THE HAUNTING OF ELENA VERA

Steven Pajak

For Paulita,
Keep the holy water
handy. You'll need it!

SP

The Haunting Of Elena Vera

Steven Pajak

The Haunting of Elena Vera

Published by Sinister Smile Press, LLC
P.O. Box 637, Newberg, OR 97132

Printed in the United States of America

Trade Paperback: 9781953112804

www.sinistersmilepress.com

ONE

Elena stood at the foot of the narrow staircase, looking up at the twenty-five steep risers leading to the attic. Her heart thudded in her small chest, and she licked her dry lips, mustering her courage to ascend the treacherous flight of stairs. Her hands trembled, threatening to drop the foil-covered plate she held in a death grip.

The staircase was frightening enough, but it was the dark and narrow corridor that awaited her at the top, leading to Uncle Milton's bedroom in the converted attic, that truly terrified Elena. Only a single dim lightbulb at the end of the hallway provided a feeble cone of illumination, around which deeply ominous shadows reigned. In her five-year-old's imagination, multitudes of horrifying and indescribable beasts hid within the darkness, coiled and ready to pounce and gut her, like when her grandmother sliced fresh fish on her cutting board and all the insides spilled out in a slimy mess.

The sound of music, laughter, and loud conversation from outside did little to ease her anxiety. Her family and close friends had gathered for some occasion she couldn't recall, yet she found no comfort in their merriment. It was she who had been burdened with braving the treacherous steps and facing unknown evils that lurked in the dark to bring food to Uncle Milton in his scary attic chamber.

Bracing herself, Elena placed her foot on the first tread, then the next, and the next, leaning her right shoulder against the wall for support as she slowly ascended. The cool, rough plaster gouged her skin beneath the thin T-shirt. She kept her eyes focused on the landing above, for fear of losing her balance should she look back. Upon reaching the landing, without hesitation, Elena bolted toward the meager source of light at the end of the hall, the flip-flops she wore making wet slapping sounds against her heels and soles of her feet as she raced along the well-worn wood floor. In her child's mind, she believed if she ran fast enough, nothing that lurked within the shadows could touch her.

She ran as fast as she could, her small voice but a breathless whisper, repeating *God protect me* until she reached the bedroom. Panting, safe now within the dirty amber hue of the single bare light bulb, Elena clutched the plate of food tightly, trying to steady her nerves and catch her breath. After a moment, she faced Uncle Milton's door. She swallowed hard, summoning what remained of her courage. She rapped on the door quickly—*knock, knock, knock*—and pushed open the door and stepped inside. She immediately noticed the temperature difference. The room was frigid when it should have been stuffy because the only window in the room was shut, and the temperature outside was nearly eighty degrees.

The bedroom was gloomy, illuminated by a single lamp that stood on the table beside the bed, which cast a dusky amber light that seemed to cut Uncle Milton in half, leaving the right side of his body and the rest of the room in rich darkness. He lay in the bed with his back propped against the headboard. He wore a sleeveless undershirt, which appeared a sickly gray. His pale legs protruded from his boxer shorts, extending out in front of him like knurled tree branches. What little hair remained atop his liver-spotted head was silver and patchy, though his eyebrows were thick and bushy, like two elderly caterpillars above his haunted brown eyes.

He did not move, nor did he acknowledge Elena when she entered. He stared blankly at the wall in front of him, as he always did. His catatonic, glazed-over eyes made Elena shiver. She did not know why her uncle was so strange or why Grandmother kept her older brother in the attic instead of sending him to the hospital where doctors could treat him as there was obviously something very wrong with him. She asked once about her uncle's condition, and Grandmother swatted her behind and sent her to her room. She never asked again.

Now, she approached the bed and held the plate out in front of her.

"I have food for you, Uncle Milt—" she began, but her words abruptly caught in her throat.

There, in the corner beside the bed, a figure stood hidden, barely visible within the shadows. Two silver eyes in the darkness peered at Elena. After a moment, the figure slowly emerged, leaning forward from the shadows and into the pale light, revealing a nightmarish woman in her eighties. Her grayish-blue skin appeared waxen and lifeless, her sunken silver eyes devoid of humanity, her hair patchy, balding in places as if she had pulled out segments in clumps. Her face was covered with webs of cracks, as if her skin were made of hardpan earth, shattered by a devastating impact. Her knurled, arthritic hands were hooked into talons that ended in thick, spade-like claws. Her mouth hinged open, revealing bile-yellow, crooked, and chipped teeth. The rancid smell of death emanated from within her.

Frozen in terror, her young mind attempting to reconcile the existence of the horrifying entity before of her, Elena could not tear her gaze away from the vile woman. Before she could react, Uncle Milton's hand shot out and grabbed her arm, his grip vice-like. The plate jolted from her fingers and shattered on the floor, its contents splattering her legs like warm shrapnel.

"It sees you, child," he croaked in Spanish, his voice hoarse with urgency. "*Run! Run and don't come back!*"

The horrifying hag's grotesque features contorted with malevolence as it shrieked and lunged for Elena, its clawed hands reaching out hungrily for tender flesh. Hot, fetid air blasted Elena's face, carrying with it the foul stench of rotted flesh and sulfur, finally breaking her paralysis.

Elena bolted from the room, her heart slamming

against her breastbone so hard she feared it would burst through her chest. She heard the scraping and gouging of the evil woman's claws against the wooden floor as it pursued her. With terror urging her forward, she sprinted for the stairs, her small feet pounding relentlessly, yet it seemed like the hallway stretched endlessly. The shadows seemed to shift and contort around her, as if mocking her escape. The evil thing was so close behind her. Just when Elena thought she could run no further, she finally reached the top of the staircase. She barreled down the steep risers, her little feet pounding against the wooden treads as she went, her fear of the demonic hag more overwhelming than her fear of falling.

But the hag was faster than expected, given her decrepit appearance. With surprising athletic agility, the evil hag sprang up onto the wall like some kind of animal, the claws on her hands and feet sinking into the pliable plaster for purchase, and then, incredibly, she scrambled across the ceiling like a demonic acrobat, her body contorting in impossible ways as she soared through the air. Her clawed, hooked fingers dug into the plaster of the walls for purchase as she slid down, leaving deep gouges in the plaster before landing in front of the horrified girl.

In a moment of panic, Elena stumbled and fell, rolling down the remaining steps to the landing below. There was sharp pain in her shoulder when she slammed against the landing at the bottom. The demon-hag descended upon her with unnatural speed, its heat searing her skin as she writhed and thrashed to escape its grasp. The demon's grotesque face drew closer, its putrid saliva splashing against Elena's lips and chin. Something slithered onto Elena's face. It felt wet and rough, like chapped skin, as it floundered over her mouth and nose. Elena struggled, but she couldn't move. She opened her mouth to scream, but it was full of something thick and solid. Its elongated tongue darted toward her, slithering into her throat, making her gag and struggle for breath. She felt the tongue flailing within her belly, as if trying to punch a hole through her guts. She gagged as it slid down her throat. It was a nightmare come to life, and Elena was helpless, on the verge of succumbing to the horror...

Elena's eyes snapped open, her body jolting upright in bed as she gasped for breath. The intense terror of the nightmare clung to her momentarily. Her heart thudded in her chest like a massive bass drum reverberating through her torso. Her hands trembled uncontrollably, and she flailed at the air in front of her, as if defending from something. A greasy sheen of sweat coated her skin, and her hair was plastered to her forehead and neck. She licked at her dry lips, trying desperately to bring moisture to them. Her heart gradually slowed when she realized she'd been dreaming.

She looked at the alarm clock; it showed 3:29, just as she had anticipated. This night terror had jolted her awake at precisely this time for nearly a week. Without intending to, her gaze shifted from the clock to the closet door, which stood ajar. She was met with a terrifying sight—a pair of gleaming silver eyes gazing at her from the closet's dark interior. Elena's fear surged in her chest like fiery heartburn, and she jumped out of bed, stumbled across the room toward the light switch, and snapped it on.

Her heart resumed thudding at an elevated pace, and her breathing quickened, as the tingle of adrenaline flushed over her as it emptied into her bloodstream. She shoved the closet door open, half-expecting whatever lurked inside to pounce on her. Light from the bedroom pushed back the shadows within, leaving only a small patch of inky darkness at the far end of the closet, below where her clothing hung. She stared into that rich pool of blackness until her eyes adjusted and the outlines of her clothing, shoe boxes, and boots became decipherable.

Hesitant, she stepped into the closet and frantically pulled the string and turned on the light. She pawed at the hanging garments to her left and then right, sweeping them back and forth to confirm nothing hid behind them. She moved further into the closet and shoved aside more hanging garments. Nothing hid among the clothes. Back in the bedroom, Elena looked around. She knew that what she saw must have been a remnant of the nightmare, that it was not real, but she also knew she couldn't rest until she was sure that nothing or no one was in the apartment.

Emboldened now, the further the horrors of the nightmare drifted from memory, she strode to the bed, got onto her knees, lifted the ends of the quilt, and peered beneath. Nothing but dust and plastic containers that housed more shoes and seasonal clothing. In the bathroom, she threw back the shower curtain, checked behind the door and in the linen closet. She moved purposefully through the kitchen and living room and found nothing out of the ordinary.

Finally, she returned to the bedroom closet and

was about to turn off the light and abandon this ridiculous search when she spied the hatch in the ceiling. The hatch opened to a pulldown ladder, which led to a small attic storage space. The realtor had told her about the extra storage when she'd shown Elena the condo, but Elena never went up there. She studied it silently, looking closely at the seam around the hatch, trying to determine whether it had been opened, if perhaps whatever she thought she saw in the closet had come from above and so had also returned.

Although she'd never opened the hatch, she'd opened others like it. The heavy springs and hinges of the ladder would have made a racket when the hatch opened into the closet and the ladder extended. Perhaps while in the throes of the nightmare she hadn't heard it open, but she certainly would have heard the ladder retract, the creak of the springs, and the scratching of wood against wood when the hatch closed.

Yet it was the only place something could have escaped to without exiting the closet. And it was the only place she had not searched. For a fraction of a second, she entertained the idea of searching the space above and immediately dismissed the horrible idea with extreme prejudice. There was no way she was insane enough to check up there right now. Maybe not even during the cold light of day, for that matter.

Leaving the closet light on, Elena backed out and closed the door. She sat on the bed for a couple of minutes, listening intensely for the slightest sound from within and staring intently at the crack of illumination between the bottom of the door and the floor, subconsciously expecting to see the line of light broken by the shadow of something moving around inside. Eventually, she glanced at the nightstand clock, and saw it was 3:47. She stared again at the crack of illumination seeping through the gap below the closet door for a few more uneventful minutes before getting up.

In the kitchen, she brewed half a pot of coffee and leaned on the counter, peering down the hall toward her bedroom while she waited, not really expecting to see anything emerge from her bedroom, but she felt strongly she needed to remain vigilant. When the coffee was ready, she poured a cup and then went to the living room. She lowered herself into the comfy chair, tucking her legs under her rather than lounging on the sofa because it gave her a line of sight to the short corridor that led to her bedroom, giving her a better viewing angle should something emerge from the closet and come in search of her.

Stop it, she scolded herself. *You're being paranoid. It was just a nightmare.*

As she sipped her coffee, she turned on the TV, more for company than distraction. She accessed a streaming network and put on the next episode of *New Girl*, although she'd watched every episode of every season ten times over. It was her comfort show, and right now she needed Jess, Nick, Schmidt, and Winston for companionship.

Two

The alarm on Elena's phone blared at seven o'clock in the morning. Groggily, she reached out and fumbled with the device, pressing the screen until the incessant alarm ceased. Slowly, like a woman thrice her age suffering from sciatica, she pushed herself upright in the chair where she had eventually dozed off just before dawn, only to be greeted by an unpleasant soreness in her shoulders and neck. With a low groan (also like a woman thrice her age), she massaged the stiff muscles, feeling exhaustion seep into her bones.

She glanced at the television and saw *New Girl* played on, several episodes ahead of where she last remembered watching. The autoplay next episode feature had continued without interruption while she'd slept. Leaning forward, Elena cradled her face in her hands, rubbing her temples vigorously. Her eyes stung with fatigue, and her head throbbed as if it had developed a rhythm of its own. She briefly contemplated calling in sick to work, but it was too late to arrange a substitute, and she'd also promised to give Carrie a ride to work while her car was in the shop.

Despite feeling utterly drained, Elena's sense of responsibility compelled her to carry on. Reluctantly, she dragged herself through the quickest shower in history, hastily washing her body but neglecting to tend to her hair. The thought of blow-drying or styling it seemed like an insurmountable task.

Standing in front of the closet, Elena hesitated briefly before boldly entering, snatching a T-shirt with the school's logo screened across the chest and a pair khaki pants from their hangers. Normally she changed in the closet, but this morning she quickly dressed in the middle of her bedroom. She swiftly pulled her hair back into a messy ponytail and left her house without brewing coffee or preparing lunch, resigned to the fact that she would have to rely on the school cafeteria for sustenance (cringe).

Twenty minutes later, she arrived at Carrie's

brownstone. It was an impressive two-story building in Edison Park with a garden apartment, which she currently rented to a young hipster who was an executive chef at a French bistro for an astronomical monthly rate. Despite being a high school teacher, Carrie Drake lived well beyond her means, thanks to the financial support from her father, one of Chicago's biggest defense attorneys whose client list included celebrities, professional athletes, and politicians. He not only provided the down payment for the property but also cosigned the loan. Carrie received a monthly stipend from him (which she jokingly referred to as a glorified allowance), and along with the collected rent and teaching salary, she enjoyed a very comfortable existence.

Casually descending the brick stoop when Elena pulled up to the curb, Carrie exuded confidence and sophistication. She wore designer jeans that accentuated her figure—leaving little to the imagination of her impressionable fifteen- and sixteen-year-old students—and a luxury cotton white-and-blue striped blouse. Her blond hair was flawlessly styled and her face done up with a full complement of makeup. In contrast, Elena felt self-conscious about her appearance. She glanced down at her plain attire, feeling a pang of insecurity. She'd barely put on lip gloss and tugged her hair into a messy ponytail.

Carrie slid into the passenger seat of Elena's modest three-year-old Honda Civic, placing her designer handbag on her lap before fastening her seatbelt. "Thanks for the ride, babe."

Elena acknowledged her with a nod and pulled away from the curb, merging into the flow of traffic. The weariness in her eyes was evident, prompting Carrie's concern. "El, did you get any sleep last night? You look like hell warmed over."

"A couple hours, I think," Elena said.

"Why couldn't you sleep? Were you thinking about Nat?" Carrie teased.

Elena's gaze shifted uneasily, and she chose her words carefully. "No, I wasn't. Natalie's ancient history, in my rearview mirror."

"Three months is hardly history, let alone ancient."

Elena shrugged. She wasn't going to be sucked into a conversation about her ex-girlfriend, especially not after such a shitty night.

"Then what?"

Elena sighed, feeling the weight of exhaustion settling upon her. "I don't know. Bad dreams."

"About...?"

"I don't remember exactly. I mean, I tried, but I lose the details almost as soon as I wake. I just know they're bad, and I can't sleep after."

Carrie was sympathetic. "I'm sorry, El. That sucks."

"It does suck."

"Maybe you need to see an oneirologist."

Elena quickly glanced at Carrie again. "A *what*? Did you make that word up?"

Carrie chuckled. "No, goof. An oneirologist is a dream doctor. Look it up if you don't believe me."

"I have a few nightmares and you immediately jump to I should see a dream shrink? A bit dramatic, don't you think?"

"If it helps you figure out your shit and get some sleep..."

Elena thought it over a moment. "I don't even remember what I dreamed. How would that even work?"

Carrie shrugged. "I don't know. I'm not an oneirologist."

Elena couldn't help but tease Carrie, eager to shift the focus away from her own troubles. "You're definitely not...*that*. What did you get your degree in again? Oh, that's right, home economics."

Carrie playfully rolled her eyes, defending her

chosen field of study. "Oh, is that supposed to be a burn? I teach very important life skills to the young and impressionable that will help them become responsible adults. Remind me what do you do?"

"I teach the *classics*. I ignite their imaginations, foster critical thinking, and shape their understanding of the world and themselves."

Carrie smirked. "So you're teaching them life lessons from the Greasers and Socs? Teaching them the fine art of rebellious thinking and how to start a rumble with words. Cause *The Outsiders* is right up there with the great masterpieces of the Greeks and Romans."

Elena laughed. "Anyway, shut up. You suck."

"Oh hey," Carrie blurted randomly and startled Elena. "Pull into the Starbucks. Your ass needs coffee right now."

"Jeez, you gave me heart palpitations," Elena said, one hand clutching at her chest. "Do we have time?"

Carrie glanced at her watch. "We have time. Don't miss the entrance."

Elena maneuvered the car into the Starbucks parking lot, finding an open spot and parking her Civic. "Do I have to go in?" she asked. "I hate this place."

Carrie, already opening her door, replied firmly, "Yes, you have to go in. Come on, get your ass out of the car."

Reluctantly, Elena dragged herself out of the vehicle. Carrie linked arms with her. "You sure you're not hungover?" Carrie teased.

"I'm positive. Just bone-weary tired."

Carrie held the door open for Elena. "I'm buying. What do you want?"

"Black coffee."

Carrie frowned playfully. "You're such a basic bitch."

"Sorry, we can't all be *sophisticated* bitches like you," Elena retorted.

Stepping into the crowded Starbucks, Elena was reminded of why she rarely stopped there for coffee. Usually, she brewed her own and carried it in a Yeti thermos, tucked into a pocket of her backpack. On the mornings she needed a cup before work but hadn't had time to brew a pot at home, she preferred the convenience of the nearby Dunkin' Donuts drive-thru—like any good basic bitch would. After what seemed like ten minutes, Carrie placed their order, and they moved aside to wait.

"Oh, did I tell you I volunteered to organize the homecoming fundraiser?" Carrie blurted. "I thought it was a good idea at the time, but now I just think, *Damn, that's a lot of work.*"

"Why did you even volunteer? You're allergic to work," Elena joked.

Carrie rolled her eyes. Countering playfully, she said, "Padding my resume, I guess."

Elena raised an eyebrow. "Be real, you volunteered because you're an attention whore."

Amused by Elena's observation, Carrie laughed. "I am!"

"Why do you need to pad your resume? Something I should know?"

"No. Just keeping my options open. You never know."

"You're not ready to move on yet, anyway."

"Why do you say that?"

"Because you haven't fucked the entire faculty yet. That's high on your bucket list, right?"

"Shit, you're right!" Carrie said and laughed. Elena joined in on the laughter but abruptly stopped when Carrie's face froze in an unsettling manner, locked in a bizarre expression.

"What are you doing?" Elena asked, when Carrie remained that way for several seconds.

Carrie did not respond and remained unmoving.

"Carrie, stop. Why are you doing that?"

Elena looked around, curious if anyone was watching them. The rest of the patrons in the Starbucks were all inert, including the baristas. Like Carrie, they were as stationary as statues. Some stood in strange postures, defying gravity, as if they were in motion when they were abruptly immobilized, like a bizarre flash mob. Panicking, Elena screamed, but no sound came from her mouth.

The world around her became a surreal nightmare as the room plunged into chaos. The overhead lights flickered, then grew steadily brighter and brighter, far beyond the output the bulbs should have been capable of producing, glowing intensely like miniature suns, before the bulbs exploded in unison, showering the area with shards of glass. The cappuccino machine hissed menacingly, spewing scalding steam and froth.

Carrie's appearance suddenly twisted grotesquely. The corners of her mouth stretching into a horrifying grin, distending her cheeks higher than should have been possible, to the point her eyes were mere slits below her brows. Her lips cracked and split open, spilling putrid yellowish puss over rows of sharp teeth that belonged in the maw of a beast, not a person. She spoke in a language Elena did not recognize or understand, her voice inhuman, animalistic.

"*Caro mea est. Animam hanc petivi.*"

Elena recoiled and involuntarily stepped backward.

"*Caro mea est. Animam hanc petivi,*" Carrie repeated in a voice not her own. Then again, louder, "*Caro mea est. Animam hanc petivi.*" And then a fourth time, in a booming voice that reverberated through Elena's chest cavity and made her cover her ears. "*CARO MEA EST! ANIMAM HANC PETIVI!*"

Carrie's mouth flopped open as if on a well-oiled hinge, the lower jaw falling against her chest, like the mandible had completely detached itself from her skull. Two blackened, pulsating appendages, each ending in twin heads of eyeless snakes, propelled from her gaping maw, targeting Elena, who screamed and flung herself backward, her arms reflexively protecting her face, and plowed into one of the tables, knocking it hard against the wall. The sound of the room abruptly crashed over her like a massive sound wave, overwhelming her senses and heightening her confusion.

Carrie stood beside her, one hand clutching Elena's elbow. Her face was normal. There was concern in her voice. "Oh my God, are you okay?"

Elena's mind reeled as it attempted to negotiate reality from the inexplicable. She pulled her arm away from Carrie and took a few unsteady steps. "Sorry, I'm so sorry, I—I—I need some air."

She rushed out of the Starbucks, barely registering Carrie calling after her or the curious glances from the patrons. Finding refuge in her car, Elena clutched the steering wheel tightly, trembling with fear and bewilderment. Her breathing became erratic as she struggled to process the unfathomable horrors she had witnessed. With her eyes squeezed shut, she attempted to calm herself, but the shocking event lingered like a dark cloud in her mind.

Carrie eventually joined her in the car, bringing with her the ordered drinks. "El, what the hell happened? You totally freaked the— Jesus, you're pale as a sheet."

Elena was too overwhelmed to explain what had just happened. She felt unable to put the unspeakable experience into words, convinced Carrie wouldn't believe her if she dared share the truth. Instead, Elena offered a halfhearted explanation, blaming her turmoil on stress and anxiety. She apologized for alarming Carrie, attempting to downplay the severity of the situation. But Carrie saw through her facade.

"El, what happened back there...that wasn't from stress or anxiety. That *wasn't* a panic attack. You saw something...*reacted* to something in there, and it *terrified* you."

Doubtful and unable to comprehend the surreal events herself, Elena couldn't find the words to convey the true horror she had experienced. Instead, she remained silent, torn between the fear of judgment and her need to share the inexplicable with her friend.

Carrie persisted. "Tell me what's happening."

"Just a panic attack."

"*Bullshit.* That was *not* a panic attack. That...that was a *psychological* attack."

Elena remained silent.

Carrie put a hand on Elena's shoulder, and her tone softened. "You know you can talk to me, El. Whatever's happening, I won't judge."

Carrie's hand on her shoulder offered comfort, and the promise of understanding created a flicker of hope in Elena's heart. Still, the weight of her experience was too heavy to bear, and she couldn't find the strength to confide in Carrie at that moment.

"I can't," Elena finally admitted, her voice heavy with emotion. "At least not now."

Respecting Elena's need for time, Carrie nodded,

offering unwavering support. "Okay. But whenever you're ready, I'm here for you."

Feeling a sense of relief that Carrie didn't push further, Elena managed a small nod. "Thank you," she whispered, the gratitude evident in her eyes.

Handing the drinks to Elena, Carrie gently insisted, "You're in no shape to drive. Switch places."

Elena knew Carrie was right. They swapped seats, and as Carrie drove the rest of the way to Northside College Prep, Elena's thoughts churned with the weight of the inexplicable nightmare that had just invaded her reality.

THREE

ELENA SAT IN THE DARK AT THE FAR CORNER OF THE classroom, lost in her thoughts. The recent recurring nightmares she experienced as of late were an unwelcome intrusion in her life, and although she did not understand their source or reason for repeating nightly, they were harmless, for the most part. At worst, she lost sleep and dragged her ass for most of the day. The manifestation of her nightmare when she was awake, though, was completely terrifying and profoundly disturbing.

The hallucination at the Starbucks—that's what it had to have been, a hallucination—had been so vivid, felt so tangible in the moment she experienced it that she was almost convinced it *was* real.

She knew that was impossible, that the experience went against the laws of nature and physics, and against the very fabric of reality. This realization was unsettling because it could only mean that there was something seriously wrong with her mind. In other words, she was losing her shit.

There was a history of mental illness in her family, at least on her mother's side. Her uncle Milton had suffered from some form of undiagnosed dementia most of his life. Elena didn't remember much about him because he died when she was very young; she and her mother had moved from Ecuador to the United States shortly after he'd passed more than twenty years ago. She only remembered that he was a strange man that never left his attic bedroom. *Abuela* bathed him twice weekly and tended to his overall hygiene. She prepared meals for him, which the family took turns delivering to his room.

Elena recalled the long, steep staircase that led to Milton's room. She had a clear visualization of it in her mind, and when she closed her eyes, she saw it as clearly as if she were back at her grandmother's home in Ecuador. The stairs were a weathered silver-gray, worn down from years of foot traffic. The risers were steep and ascended into darkness. A sense of dread welled up inside her, as it did when she was a young girl. An immediate tension constricted her chest as the image of the staircase ignited her memory, and the details of the recurring nightmare crashed over her.

The dream flashed through her mind in snippets: the ominous staircase, bolting across the dark hallway, Uncle Milton on the bed with an expressionless look on his face, and then the thing in the corner...the hag with silver eyes and spade-like claws reaching for her and the bloodcurdling shriek...

A sudden chill enveloped the room, and Elena shivered, her hands unconsciously rubbing the sides of her arms, which broke out into goosebumps. The temperature in the room plummeted, and vapor escaped her lips when she exhaled.

"What the hell?" she whispered to herself.

She observed her students for their reaction to the sudden drop in temperature. They were all motionless, staring blankly at the screen at the front of the room where the film adaptation of *The Outsiders* was projected onto the pulldown screen. The lighting from the movie cast strange shadows across their faces, shifting from white and blue to deep red, painting their faces in bloody color tones.

Elena stood up and walked around to the front of

her desk. Awash in bright light from the projector, she raised her arm to shade her eyes and crossed the room to the first row of desks. She attempted to get the attention of Manny, a tow-headed boy with thick glasses who like to draw in the margins of his notebooks during class. She snapped her fingers in front of him, but he did not respond, didn't even blink an eye. She moved to the next student, Maria, one of her brightest students, and waved her hands in front of the girl—yet again, no response.

Fear exploded in her belly like sour acid, radiating out to her limbs. Her legs felt weak, and her hands trembled. Doing her best not to panic, Elena grasped Maria's shoulders and shook her gently, hoping to elicit a response from the catatonic teen.

The sound of the film transformed suddenly, and the dialog between Ponyboy and Soda Pop faded, replaced by raspy, heavy breathing. Turning slowly, Elena faced the screen. The projector flickered and wavered, casting twisted and contorted images around her that bore no resemblance to *The Outsiders*. Panic surged through Elena's veins, and her breath caught in her throat as the demon-hag materialized before her, a macabre apparition on screen. Elena's body tensed. The sinister gaze of the hag locked onto Elena's own, sending shivers down her spine. She felt a cold sweat forming on her brow, her heart beating wildly against her ribs like a caged bird desperate for escape.

With a chilling shriek that reverberated through the room, the demon-hag emerged, one leg breaking through the barrier of the two-dimensional world on screen and materializing into the classroom right in front of Elena's eyes. The demon's bare foot made a wet, smacking sound against the tile floor, then the rest of its corporeal body followed, dropping with a meaty thud to the floor behind the desk, out of Elena's line of sight.

Acute fear overwhelmed Elena like a flash of heat, and she stood frozen in a state of mild shock and denial. *This is not happening,* she attempted to convince herself. *This is just a hallucination. Your mind is sick. This isn't real.*

Steeling herself, Elena approached the desk and placed both hands on the Formica top and leaned forward far enough so that she could see the floor on the opposite side. She held her breath in anticipation and let it out in a deep sigh when she saw nothing sinister lurked there.

Get ahold of yourself, Elena.

The biting chill in the room persisted, and the hairs on the back of her neck raised like hackles. A sharp scrape of a chair leg against the tile floor drew her attention, and she spun to face the class, hoping briefly that the sound meant the students were no longer catatonic, that the hallucination had ended.

The demon-hag slithered down the center of the aisle between the rows of desks; her horrible, claw-like fingers intertwined into Marty Detwieler's mop of shaggy brown hair. The hag dragged the boy from his chair and across the floor as she sluggishly came toward Elena. As the hag walked, her bare feet slapping sickly against the tile, she extended her other hand, raking her claws across the faces and necks of the seated children. Blood oozed or spurted from torn flesh and flayed arteries, but the kids remained motionless, seemingly paralyzed and unaware of their fate.

"Stop it!" Elena screamed, her emotions spiraling into chaos, torn between the urge to flee and the desperate need to protect her students.

But before she could take a single step, the demon-hag flickered and disappeared, then instantly materialized right before Elena, her grotesque face mere inches away. The stench of decay filled the air, and a surge of nausea washed over Elena. In a horrifying instant, the demon-hag lunged at Elena, her claws slashing through the air like blades of darkness. Elena's heart pounded in her ears and her breath caught in her throat as she narrowly evaded the attack, ducking away and side-stepping to her right.

Fighting back a cresting tide of panic, Elena's eyes fixated on the classroom door. Escape became her sole obsession, her mind fixated on reaching the safety of the outside world and at the same time drawing the danger away from her classroom. With a surge of adrenaline, she sprinted toward the exit, the hope of salvation propelling her forward. With an unholy force, the demon-hag shoved Elena from behind and sent her crashing into the door. Agonizing pain erupted in her head, and her vision blurred as she crumpled to the floor, her world spinning into darkness.

Haunted by the hag's maniacal laughter, Elena struggled to remain conscious. The room warped and twisted around her, as the oblivious students gathered in concern, their faces a blur of worry. Elena's mind was consumed by the horrifying encounter.

"Someone go get Ms. Drake!" Maria's voice cut through the chaos, her fear and determination palpable. Her classmates rushed for help, and she took a deep breath and spoke more calmly. "Don't move, Ms. Vera. You hit your head pretty hard, and there's some blood."

Lying on the cold classroom floor with her head cradled in Maria's arms, Elena heard the beating of the poor girl's heart, like her own pulse throbbing through her ear. The classroom felt eerily quiet—someone had paused the movie and turned on the lights—except for the soft sound of her own shallow breaths and the terrified whispers from the students who had witnessed the unsettling scene.

Elena closed her eyes, mortified.

Anxious footsteps echoed through the hallway, and seconds later, Carrie entered the classroom. She stopped, her eyes darting across the room, noting the flipped desks and terrified students. She swallowed hard, then saw Elena on the floor and knelt beside her.

"Let me see," she told Maria and began to examine Elena's head wound. "Shit, you're bleeding, babe." She looked at Maria. "Get some tissues from her desk. I've got her."

Reluctantly, Maria shifted out from under Elena,

and Carrie slid her arm under to support her and then helped her sit up. "Jesus, El, what happened?"

Elena attempted to touch the wound on her head, but Carrie gently guided her hand away. Maria returned with a box of tissues, which she set on the floor. She snatched several tissues from the box and applied them gently and winced when Elena made a hissing sound.

"Sorry!"

"Maria, what happened?" Carrie eyed the girl.

"I don't really know..." Maria hesitated, looking to Elena for guidance.

Elena felt light-headed, embarrassed, and confused. She forced herself to sit further up, pushing one leg under her and one hand placed against the floor.

"I'm fine," she said, feeling a flush of heat in her cheeks. Her head throbbed, and the spot on her head where she'd slammed into the door itched like hell for some reason. "I just need someone to help me up."

Carrie stood, and together with Maria, they hoisted Elena to her feet. She swayed momentarily. Maria wrapped an arm around her waist to steady her. "I think you should sit down, Ms. Vera."

Mr. Smart, Northside College Prep's principal,

entered the room at a run. He bent forward, one hand on his knee and the other gripping a walkie talkie. Breathless, he asked, "Is anyone hurt? Do we need security or medical assistance?" His head seemed to be on a swivel as he surveyed the state of the room.

"Elena has a small cut on her head, but I think everyone else is okay," Carrie said.

"Lord," Mr. Smart said. His free hand now clutched his chest. "Get her to my office. Maria, help Ms. Drake. Is anyone else hurt?"

The students all shook their heads, and Mr. Smart sighed, visibly relieved that there weren't casualties. When he heard that there was a commotion in one of the classrooms, his mind had immediately gone to an active shooter situation or classroom brawl, which had been very real threats at the previous Chicago public school where he served as assistant principal before coming to Northside College Prep.

"Kids, listen up! Please start organizing the room. I'll have a teacher come in shortly. Until then, please clean up. And behave!"

Carrie and Maria walked Elena to Mr. Smart's office while he went to fetch someone to take over Elena's classroom. Thankfully, it was the last period of the day, and the school day was mostly over.

In the office, Elena slowly lowered herself into one of the chairs in front of the desk. She insisted she was fine, but Carrie asked Maria to get the nurse anyway. "And then go back to class."

Maria paused at the door; obviously invested in Elena's wellbeing, she wanted to stay.

"Thank you, Maria," Carrie said and watched the girl until she was out of sight. She knelt in front of her friend, placing both hands on Elena's knees, and lowered her voice. "Did it happen again? Like this morning?"

Elena still clutched the wadded tissues against her head. She pulled it away and looked at it and winced. "I'm not feeling too great right now. Can we talk about this later?"

"Mike's not going to wait until later for an explanation, El."

As if he possessed an uncanny sense to appear when his name was spoken, Mr. Smart appeared with the school nurse in tow. "Elena, let Maggie take a look at you, please."

Carrie stood and moved out of the way, allowing Nurse Maggie to do her thing. She stood next to Mr. Smart, who silently observed with his hands crossed over his chest. Dark sweat patches stained the armpits of his polo. The walkie talkie was clipped to his belt. His posture and the thick Magnum, P. I. mustache perched over his lip gave off extreme cop vibes.

Nurse Maggie finished cleaning the wound, which wasn't very deep and had stopped bleeding. She dressed it with a small compression bandage. "I'm all done here, but I strongly suggest you go to the hospital straightaway. The cut is minor, but you need to be examined for concussion. Head trauma is serious business."

"Thank you," Elena said, knowing full well a trip to the emergency room was not happening.

After Maggie departed, Mr. Smart sat at the edge of his desk directly across from Elena, and Carrie plopped down in the seat beside her. Elena suddenly felt like a child whose parents were ready to admonish her for poor behavior.

"How are you feeling?" Mr. Smart asked. "Any pain?"

"No. I'm just feeling a bit tired."

"Hmm. That's not good for a head wound," he said. He looked to Carrie for confirmation.

"He's right. Don't they say after a head wound, you shouldn't go to sleep?"

Elena held up her hands. "I just said I'm tired, but I won't fall asleep. I promise."

Mr. Smart uncrossed his arms and gripped the edge of his desk with both hands. Leaning forward slightly, a sympathetic look crossing his face, he asked Elena, "So what happened in your classroom?"

Elena expected the question. How could she not? Both Carrie and Mr. Smart seemed baited, desperate for an explanation she knew she could not give, at least not the truth.

"To be honest, I think I had a panic attack. I just suddenly started feeling very warm, and then it was hard to breathe, and my ears started ringing. I just needed some air. I ran for the door and got a bit woozy and fell into it. That's how I hit my head."

Mr. Smart stared at her for a good several seconds—*He smells bullshit*, Elena thought—an intimidation tactic he employed often when dealing with troublemakers. Finally, he said, "The kids were really frightened, Elena. Terrified, actually."

Elena shook her head. Avoiding eye contact, she said, "I can only imagine. I mean, I'm sure the way I jumped and ran toward the door must have been unexpected."

Crossing his arms over his chest again, Mr. Smart

leaned in. "They said you were screaming at something that wasn't there. That you looked like...you were fending something off."

"That's just...that's not right," Elena scoffed. "That's exaggerated."

"Several students gave a corroborated description of what they saw."

Elena put her hands in her lap and started to unconsciously pick at a piece of loose skin at the corner of her thumbnail.

Carrie put a hand on Elena's arm and leaned over. "El, I think you should tell him about this morning."

Elena looked sharply at Carrie. "How dare you bring that up?"

Surprised by Elena's abrupt anger, Carrie took her hand away and leaned back in the chair.

"What's this now?" Mr. Smart asked, looking from Carrie to Elena and back again.

"Don't I have a right to privacy?" Elena snipped. "I don't appreciate you getting into my personal business with her in the room."

"Elena, are you for real right now?" Carrie protested.

Mr. Smart looked toward Carrie and held his hand up. His voice was edged with a note of urgency.

"Carrie, please give us a moment alone." His tone left no room for negotiation.

Carrie hesitated, clearly reluctant to leave her friend, but under Mr. Smart's firm nod, she had no choice but to comply, leaving the room with a backward glance of worry.

When Carrie was gone, Mr. Smart turned his attention back to Elena, his tone now gentle but insistent. "Elena, I need to know what happened in your classroom."

Elena took a deep breath and finally looked him in the eyes. She said, "I had a panic attack. I needed some fresh air. I must have hit my head when I rushed for the door."

Mr. Smart sighed, clearly dissatisfied with her response. He took a long pause, considering how he should proceed. In a stern, official tone he reserved for disciplinary matters, he said, "Elena, clearly something happened that you are uncomfortable discussing with me. I understand that it can be difficult to discuss personal matters. But the fact is you disrupted your class, put the fear of God into your students—although unintentionally, I believe. The kids are telling me one thing and you're telling me something else."

Standing up from the desk, he moved behind it

and sat down in his chair. "The safety of the student body, of the faculty, of everyone on the premises, is my responsibility." He paused again, leaning forward on his desk and intertwining his fingers. "Elena, I'm sorry, but I'm putting you on temporary medical leave until you can provide a doctor's note stating you are in good health and not a danger to yourself or others."

"Mike, this is ridiculous," Elena scoffed. "I think you're blowing things out of proportion. You can't force me to go to a doctor."

"I'm not forcing you to do anything. What you do is up to you. But as of right now, you are no longer allowed on the premises or in front of a classroom until you can present me with documentation from a board-certified physician that you are not a danger to these kids or yourself."

"Mike, please—"

"The conversation is over, Elena. You obviously disagree with me, but my decision is final. You're welcome to contact your union representative to seek recourse, but until then, do not return to work. You are on forced medical leave, with pay, until further notice."

Elena was stunned, rendered speechless. A knot of dread dropped in her stomach as she rose to her feet. She started to speak, but she knew arguing wouldn't change Mr. Smart's decision. Feeling defeated and overwhelmed, Elena left the office without another word. Her mind was in turmoil, unsure of what to do next. She leaned against the corridor wall, trying to process the situation.

"This is fucking unreal," she whispered to herself, her arms clutching her stomach as though she were going to be sick. So much had happened in less than twenty-four hours, and she felt powerless to stop whatever was happening.

She returned to her classroom and peered through the window. Mr. Hutchins, the PE teacher, sat behind the desk with his feet kicked up, monitoring the class as they continued to screen *The Outsiders*. It all seemed eerily normal, yet just minutes ago the class had been entwined in a supernatural encounter. She entered the room as quietly as she could and went straight to the desk. She grabbed her handbag that hung over the back of the chair. Mr. Hutchins got out of the seat and watched uncomfortably as she opened her desk drawer, hastily gathering her personal items, and left without a word.

She exited the classroom and started down the hall in the direction of the parking lot when Carrie stepped out from her classroom and called out to her, her voice filled with concern. But Elena was not ready to face her, the taste of betrayal still fresh in her mind. She quickened her pace, hurrying down the corridor toward the exit, and Carrie followed.

FOUR

MARIA LEANED AGAINST MS. VERA'S CAR, CHEWING nervously at her fingernails, a habit her mother had been trying to break since she was a toddler by putting hot sauce on her fingertips. Right now, her thoughts were consumed by the ordeal that had unfolded in front of the entire class. She was deeply concerned for Ms. Vera. Maria could only imagine how embarrassed and overwhelmed Ms. Vera must feel after such a meltdown in front of the students. She couldn't help but think about the heartlessness of her classmates and how callous they were afterward. None of them showed any sympathy and instead made jokes and mimicked the poor woman. Maria wouldn't be surprised if one or more of her classmates recorded the episode and had already posted it on TikTok. These assholes didn't care about anyone's feelings or the repercussions of their actions.

When Ms. Vera finally exited the building, Ms. Drake ran behind her trying to catch up. It was pretty clear from her body language that Ms. Vera was pissed at Ms. Drake about something that must have happened after Ms. Drake sent Maria away.

"Elena, damn it, *stop.*"

Elena stopped and whirled on Carrie with a ferocity that stopped Carrie in her tracks and made her take a step back.

"How dare you bring up what happened this morning in front of Mike?"

"Come on, El," Carrie said in a hushed voice. "You had a full-blown *freak out* in front of your kids. How was I *not* going to tell Mike about what happened earlier? Besides, I shouldn't have had to be the one to say something."

"You're right. It was *my* place to tell him, not yours. And obviously I didn't want to, or I would have. Now because you opened your damn mouth, I'm on forced leave. Thank you for that."

"Shit," Carrie said. "I'm sorry, El, I didn't think—"

"Yeah, you didn't." Elena shook her head. "You

just can't help yourself. You always have to insert yourself in everyone's business and make shit worse."

"El, I think you're being a bit—"

Elena didn't let her finish. "Just fuck off!" she shouted and stormed away.

Carrie was stunned into silence for a moment before she called out, "Elena, you're my ride!"

Without looking back, Elena yelled, "Call an Uber!"

Seething, Elena's hands shook as she dug the key fob from her purse. Approaching her car, she spotted Maria. She held up her hand before Maria could speak and said, "I am *not* in the mood right now."

"I'm sorry," Maria apologized. "I just wanted to make sure you were okay."

"Don't worry about it. Go back to class. You shouldn't be out here."

Maria hesitated, then asked, "What happened to you this morning? I overheard—"

"That's none of your business," Elena snapped.

"I just thought maybe you wanted to talk about it with someone—"

"If I wanted to talk to someone, it wouldn't be

with a child. Go back inside before you get detention."

Elena yanked open the car door and threw her bag inside. She paused with one hand on the frame of the door and the other on the roof of the car, then took a deep breath and looked at Maria. "I'm sorry. I know you're just trying to help, but right now I just need to be alone."

"It's okay," Maria said.

"And I appreciate what you did for me in the classroom. You were very kind. Now go back inside before you get in trouble." Elena got into the car, started the ignition, and then drove off.

Maria remained in the parking lot for a moment. Her heart was filled with dread for Ms. Vera. If what she thought was wrong with Ms. Vera was true, then she desperately needed help whether she wanted it or not.

FIVE

LATER THAT EVENING, CARRIE LAY ON THE SOFA, A light throw blanket draped over her legs. She sipped a glass of wine while an episode of *Beat Bobby Flay* played on television, though she wasn't really watching. The events of the day weighed heavily on her mind, and she couldn't stop thinking about Elena and how things were left between them. A suffocating guilt gnawed at her; she knew she had grossly mishandled the situation earlier. Although her actions came from a place of love and deep concern for her friend, she should have left it to Elena to decide who she wanted to share and with whom. Carrie had been calling Elena incessantly since she left school in a ride share, hoping to apologize and make things right.

For the past three years, they had been classroom neighbors and close friends, bonding instantly when they first met. They had weathered their fair share of disagreements over the years, like any true friends did, but nothing compared to the intensity of this afternoon's events. Carrie knew Elena was going through some personal struggles and perhaps even some mental challenges, and she should have been more compassionate and understanding and respectful of her privacy. The fact that Elena was avoiding her calls only added to Carrie's anxiety, making it impossible for her to enjoy her evening.

Carrie set her wine glass on the table and checked her phone for the umpteenth time. More than an hour had passed since her last attempt to reach Elena. Feeling restless and suffocated by her guilt, she opened the phone app to her favorites and dialed Elena's number yet again. The phone rang three times before, surprisingly, Elena answered.

"Oh my God, Elena, I've been trying to reach you all evening," Carrie babbled apologetically. "I am so sorry—"

Elena immediately cut her off, her response anything but warm. Her voice sounded strange, deep, and phlegmy, as she replied, "I don't want to talk to you. Stop calling."

Carrie's heart sank. "Okay, I get it. You're upset but—"

"Do you get it, you annoying twat? Because it seems like you don't. I mean, if you call someone twenty times and they don't pick up, maybe you should get a fucking clue and realize *they don't want to talk to you!*"

"Christ, El, you don't have to be such a jerk—"

A sharp shriek pierced Carrie's ear through the phone, causing her to drop it in surprise. She quickly scrambled to pick it up, almost knocking the wine glass over when she bumped the table in her haste. Her heart pounded in her chest when she brought the phone back to her ear.

"El, are you there?" She was greeted by an eerie chorus of voices, overlapping and indistinguishable, as if thousands of people were talking all at once. "El, what is that noise?"

Carrie's confusion and fear grew as she tried to make sense of what was happening. The chaotic voices continued, making it impossible to understand any single word. A chant formed, and she realized the same several words were being repeated, though they were foreign to her. The hundreds of voices began to grow in volume and intensity.

"Caro mea est... Caro mea est... Caro mea est...CARO MEA EST...CARO MEA EST!"

Carrie pulled the phone away from her ear, the cries of the legion almost bursting her eardrum. Then suddenly, the phone disconnected, and the screen went blank.

"What the hell?"

She stared at the phone in her hand as if she expected it to come alive again with a chorus of a hundred scratchy voices. She finally set the phone on the table and pulled the throw blanket over her body, suddenly feeling gooseflesh break out across her bare arms.

Was this some kind of prank? she wondered. *A tasteless joke to get back at me for what I said in Mike's office?*

Uncertainty gnawed at her, and a profound sense of foreboding settled over her. Something was terribly wrong, and she couldn't shake the feeling that there was more going on with Elena than what she witnessed today. Her instincts told her that Elena was in deep distress, and she needed to find a way to reach out and help her, no matter how difficult it might be.

Six

THE RECURRING NIGHTMARE AND THE TERRIFYING hallucinations this morning and afternoon all but consumed Elena's thoughts, gnawed at her mind with voracity, leaving her disturbed and edgy. As the evening wore on, the deep unease grew, fueled by her curiosity about the storage space above her closet. She couldn't shake the feeling that something awaited her there—a truth that was somehow connected and she needed to expose.

Elena mechanically prepared a dinner of oven-roasted chicken breast and garden salad. She sat at the kitchen island staring blankly out the living room window. The food grew cold as she pushed it around the plate, her appetite having waned. The shrill ring of her phone shattered the uncomfortable silence, but she ignored it, knowing it was Carrie calling again. She tossed the uneaten food from the plate into the trash, then quickly placed the leftovers into containers and shoved them into the refrigerator.

She retrieved her MacBook, intending to review her students' *The Outsiders* book reports, when she remembered she was on forced leave and temporarily (she hoped) relieved of her teaching responsibilities. Frustrated, she closed the lid and set the MacBook aside and turned on the television, tuning into *New Girl*, picking up at the episode where she'd left off last night.

The sudden ringing of her phone jolted her. Annoyed, she silenced the ringer—thinking, *Stop fucking calling me, bitch*—and turned the phone face down on the table.

A moment later, she found herself standing at the threshold of the closet door. A small two-step folding ladder leaned against the wall, and she held a flashlight in her hand; she had no memory of getting up from the sofa, retrieving these two items from the hall closet, and walking to her room. Darkness pressed against the bedroom windows, and Elena glanced at the clock, stunned to see it was after three in the morning.

How the hell did I lose so much time? she thought. *How long have I been standing here?*

A knot of raw fear formed in Elena's belly like a tart Sour Patch Kid. Perplexed, Elena entered the closet and flicked on the light. She looked up at the storage hatch, knowing in her gut that something was guiding her (compelling her?) to search that unknown space. Moving quickly before fear and doubt took over, she unfolded the ladder, positioning it carefully in front of the hatch, giving herself enough room for it to swing open into the closet. With a deep breath, she grasped the small rope and pulled.

The hatch resisted, barely yielding to her efforts. She exerted more force, her muscles straining. Suddenly, the hatch gave way, swinging down with great force, narrowly missing her face. Simultaneously, the ladder snapped open abruptly, crashing into the step ladder she perched upon and knocking her backward.

Elena found herself sprawled on the floor, gazing up into the abyss above her. The perfect darkness seemed impenetrable, impervious to the closet light. Her heart pounded in her chest, its rhythm matching her racing thoughts. She located the flashlight on the floor beside her and switched it on, the crisp white beam slicing through the chilling darkness above.

The light illuminated the wooden rafters and the roof vents, revealing a desolate space above. Gathering her resolve, Elena rose to her feet, standing at the base of the ladder. One rung at a time, she ascended, her heart pounding louder in her ears with each step.

As she approached the opening above, her head just below the rectangular void, a chilling realization washed over her. The sheer anticipation of what might await her in the dark chasm intensified her fear. The feeling of the unknown seeped into her bones, causing her throat to constrict. Swallowing hard, she placed her right foot on the next rung, gripping the ladder with one hand and clutching the flashlight tightly in the other.

With a surge of determination, Elena pushed herself upward, her head and the flashlight emerging through the opening simultaneously. Sweeping the flashlight's beam from left to right, her eyes darted around the room, searching for any signs of the unearthly.

Her heart hammered against her ribcage, threatening to burst as she pivoted on the ladder, training the flashlight behind her. The harsh beam illuminated stacks of dust-covered two-by-fours and left-over building supplies, dispelling any immediate danger. Yet an unshakable sense of unease smothered her, mingled with the faint smell of sulfur that permeated the air.

Sudden movement caught her attention—a swift motion from left to right, as if something ran past. Her grip tightened on the flashlight as she swung it toward the direction of the perceived movement, her breath hitching in anticipation. But there was nothing—only the ominous presence of the silent attic. Now she sensed movement behind her, a fleeting presence that sent a shiver down her spine. She spun around again, gripping the flashlight tightly in her trembling hand. But there was nothing there, just a maze of old wooden beams and discarded debris.

Something was toying with her or her mind was playing tricks on her, conjuring sinister shapes in the darkness. Every creak and groan of the dusty, neglected attic intensified her overwhelming fear. She swept the flashlight across the attic, desperate for reassurance that she was alone. But her hopes were shattered when the light revealed something in the far corner—an unsettling sight that froze her in place.

Her breath caught in her throat as the beam illuminated a pair of dirty, scraped feet protruding from the shadows. A sense of foreboding gripped her, suffusing her with a primal terror. She dared not move; her eyes fixated on the figure before her. As the light crept slowly upward, revealing a soiled sleeping gown and a face obscured by dirty, stringy hair, Elena's pulse accelerated. The woman's features were haggard, her eyes sunken and filled with determined malice. A muffled gasp escaped Elena's lips, but before she could react, the silence of the murky attic was shattered by a bloodcurdling screech emanating from the twisted mouth of the decrepit woman. With lightning speed, the hag sprinted toward Elena on all fours like a rabid bear, her movements unnatural and jerky. Panic surged through Elena, and she involuntarily recoiled in such absolute terror that she lost her footing on the rickety ladder.

Time seemed to slow as Elena tumbled backward, the back of her head colliding brutally with the sharp edge of the attic opening. Pain exploded through her skull, disorienting her. As she plummeted toward the floor, the flashlight slipped from her grasp, casting wild beams of light across the room. It bounced against the wall and then rolled back toward her, its feeble glow offering a glimpse of the nightmare unfolding.

Lying on the floor, dazed and disoriented, Elena struggled to regain her bearings. The ringing in her ears drowned out all other sound. Her vision blurred, and a sluggish lethargy seeped through her body. She fought against the encroaching darkness, forcing her eyes to stay open.

Through the haze, she gazed up at the pitch-black void above her, where silence engulfed the attic. Fear clenched her heart as she realized she was powerless at the mercy of the unknown. The stillness was shattered by a sudden movement—a pair of silver eyes glinting in the darkness above with a malevolent hunger.

In that split second, Elena's breath caught in her throat, paralyzed by terror. The hag, her twisted form contorting unnaturally, scuttled down the first several rungs of the ladder before hurtling down from the darkness, landing atop Elena with an earth-shattering force. Pain exploded through Elena's body as the demon-hag's gnarled fingers closed around her throat, cutting off her screams.

Panicked, Elena gasped for air that would not come. She slapped at the foul woman's arms and ineffectively pried at its grip. The world faded into a nightmarish haze as the hag's silver eyes bore into Elena's soul. In that final moment of terror, her mind screamed for escape, but it was too late. The chilling darkness swallowed her whole, leaving only the echoes of her futile struggle.

Seven

Maria dreamed of Ms. Vera.

Enveloped by a surreal stillness, she stood as a mere observer, her senses attuned to the unfolding nightmare as if trapped within a twisted cinematic reel. Ms. Vera materialized, shrouded by an oppressive darkness. A claustrophobic gloom clung to the scene, obscuring all but the upper reaches of her form—a sight that sent tremors through Maria's core.

A surreal luminescence emanated from a solitary flashlight grasped in Ms. Vera's trembling hand. Its feeble glow barely pierced the shadows, casting an eerie dance of light and darkness. When Ms. Vera engaged the flashlight, Maria saw that she was standing on a ladder, looking into the creepy, yawning attic cavity. Although not an active participant in the dream, Maria could smell dust and mildew, and something else, a foul odor that was familiar, like a cross between boiled eggs and ignited matches.

Ms. Vera swept the flashlight across the mostly barren space, pushing back the shadows within the two-foot spread of the flashlight's beam. As she swept light back to her left, it illuminated something pale and grayish. Ms. Vera froze. A pair of filth-caked feet, naked and unwholesome, materialized first, their grimy toes curling like a spider's legs. The light ascended slowly, revealing a decrepit woman, ensnared by a soiled nightgown. Her hair was dirty, matted, and covered most of her cracked, wrinkled face.

The flashlight reflected off dead eyes, long extinguished, replaced by deadened silver orbs. Maria gasped as the old woman lunged with a feral agility, knocking Ms. Vera down from the ladder. As though riding an unholy wave of malevolence to the floor, the crone landed atop Ms. Vera, who appeared to have lost consciousness. The ancient crone leaned closer, her skeletal digits prying open Ms. Vera's mouth with unholy determination. A snake-like appendage, slithering forth with an unnatural grace —Maria realized it was the *vieja's* (old woman's) tongue—into Ms. Vera's open mouth. Her cheeks puffed out and her throat bulged as the snake-tongue pushed its way inside.

As Ms. Vera's chest and stomach became distended—*That fucking thing is killing her from the inside*, Maria screamed in her mind—the disgusting *vieja* suddenly became aware of the dream passenger and the crone's head snapped to the side, her cold silver eyes locked onto Maria's, and the girl felt her blood instantly run cold. An unnatural retraction seized the snake-tongue, withdrawing it from Ms. Vera's throat with the speed of a recoiling whip. With her full attention on Maria, the *vieja* suddenly launched herself again, her claws slashing, raking across Maria's shoulder as she instinctually turned away from the horrible creature.

Maria's scream carried over from her dream and into the waking world, though the scream was not the only thing she carried back with her from the nightmare. She scrambled atop her bed, her feet kicking wildly and digging into the mattress for purchase, until her back pressed against the headboard. She clutched her blanket so hard that the tendons in her wrists began to ache, barely able to catch her breath, still completely shaken to her core, the image of the *vieja malvada* (evil woman) burned in her brain, and the deep sinking dread still clinging to her like a wet blanket.

As the tension of the nightmare slowly slipped away, Maria felt a dull throb on her left shoulder, a relentless reminder of the *vieja's* insidious attack. She gingerly slid the oversized sleeping T-shirt off her shoulder and gasped when she saw three short slash marks in the place where the *vieja* scratched her in the dream. They were not deep wounds, just surface scratches, though small dots of blood appeared along the edges of the wounds.

"*No way,*" Maria whispered incredulously in the predawn darkness of her bedroom.

Maria's family believed in *brujería* (witchcraft) and the occult. As a young girl, she'd witnessed several *limpieza espiritual* (spiritual cleansings) performed by elders skilled in the ceremonies and rituals of *La Limpia.* She'd grown up with stories of *posesión demoníaca* (demonic possession) told by her family that gave her nightmares for weeks as a young child. She shivered, realizing the stories were real, that something unspeakably evil and insidious had attached itself to Ms. Vera and soon it would consume her very soul.

Maria looked at the clock on her phone and saw it was 3:29.

EIGHT

MARIA COULDN'T FOCUS ON ANYTHING AT SCHOOL AND went through the morning in a sort of daze. She was exhausted, running on only a few hours of sleep and copious amounts of Café Bustelo she'd ingested since three-thirty in the morning. She couldn't shake the feeling of dread whenever she thought about Ms. Vera, and that was *all* she could think about since the classroom incident and now the terrifying nightmare. Unconsciously, her right hand went to her wounded shoulder, gingerly pressing against the trio of scratches that had no business being there. Scratches from an evil woman in a dream, which was impossible. Yet she knew the scores across her flesh were not self-inflicted. She'd placed her fingers over the wounds and observed in the mirror the abrasions were clearly made by nails wider than her own. *Claws.*

After fourth period, she had study hall, which she normally spent in the library *actually* studying because it was incredibly difficult to focus on schoolwork at home. Her mother placed a high priority on *responsabilidad familiar* (family responsibility), which meant helping prepare dinner, trash duty, laundry, and taking care of her younger brother who had turned two earlier this year and was an absolute terror. Today she completely lacked the ability to focus (understandably), and instead of the library, she went to Ms. Drake's class hoping to get some information about Ms. Vera. She knew the two of them were tight, and if anyone knew what Ms. Vera was going through, it would be Ms. Drake.

She found Ms. Drake in her classroom. The door was closed, but Maria saw through the window she was reading a book while munching on carrot sticks. She looked sad without her friend, and Maria felt a twinge of sympathy. She didn't want to disturb Ms. Drake during her break, but it was likely the only time she could be alone with her (and she looked like she could use some company), so it was now or never. Summoning her courage for the sake of Ms.

Vera, Maria knocked on the door, then pushed it open without waiting for an invite to enter.

Ms. Drake looked up from her novel, saw it was Maria, and looked concerned. Normally, when a student sought her out during free periods, they had something heavy on their minds.

"What is it? Is everything okay?"

"Sorry to bother you, but I was wondering...how is Ms. Vera?"

Carrie placed her bookmark carefully and set the paperback on the desk. She pushed aside the baggie of carrot sticks, appearing grateful for the interruption. "I wish I had an answer for you."

"What do you mean?" Maria inquired, stepping closer to Ms. Drake's desk. "Didn't you check on her?"

Carrie got up from her seat, gesturing for Maria to sit beside her at a desk nearby. "I tried calling her many times last night, but she wouldn't take my calls." It was mostly true, although eventually, Elena did pick up, but that conversation was too surreal to discuss with Maria. "We had a bit of a...disagreement the other day, and she's upset with me."

"I overheard some of it in the parking lot," Maria admitted, her gaze dropping to the desk.

Carrie raised an eyebrow. "I won't ask why you

were outside of the school when you should have been in class."

"I was just worried about Ms. Vera."

Carrie regarded Maria thoughtfully. "I get it. I know Elena is your favorite teacher, and I saw the way you took care of her the other day in class. She would be deeply touched to know you're here asking about her."

Maria's eyes shifted back to the desk, embarrassed by Ms. Drake's compliment. "She is my favorite teacher—and so are you, of course—but it's not just that. I'm really worried about her because there's...something really bad happening to Ms. Vera, and she needs help."

"What do you mean?" Carrie leaned over and touched Maria's hand. "If you know something about Elena that I don't, please tell me now."

Maria hesitated, searching Ms. Drake's eyes for understanding. Telling Ms. Drake that she thought Ms. Vera was being haunted by an evil entity or was cursed by *mal de ojo* (the evil eye) would only make her sound ignorant, and she'd be less likely to help her get in touch with Ms. Vera. "You wouldn't believe me if I told you."

"Tell me," Carrie said, her voice soft. "Please."

Meeting Ms. Drake's gaze once more, Maria

revealed, "What happened in the classroom to Ms. Vera, you told Mr. Smart that something like that happened to her earlier in the morning."

"How did you—" Carrie started, then remembered Maria was eavesdropping in the parking lot.

"Did she act like she was...*interacting* with someone that wasn't there?"

"Yes," Carrie said, becoming more attentive. "And whatever it was, it scared her bad. I mean she was *really* shaken."

"That's what happened in class, too. She was really scared and...it looked like she was fighting with something, and then the way she ran, it was like something horrible was after her and she was terrified."

Carrie squeezed Maria's hand. "I'm so sorry you all had to see that. I know how frightening that must have been."

"Some of the kids were laughing, like it was funny seeing Ms. Vera so afraid."

"Kids can be assholes sometimes, present company excluded, of course."

Maria was at first surprised by Ms. Drake cursing but then laughed. "Most times. Excluding present company."

Carrie smiled and gave Maria's hand another

squeeze. "What is it you're trying to tell me? You're trying to make a connection. Help me understand."

"You have to keep an open mind, Ms. Drake. I know you won't believe me, but you have to. For Ms. Vera's sake."

"Just tell me, Maria."

After a momentary pause, Maria said, "I think that an evil entity attached itself to Ms. Vera. I don't know how or why, but I know it's dangerous, and if we don't do something to help her, it could take over, possess her."

Carrie fell into a momentary silence, carefully choosing her words before responding. She didn't want to invalidate Maria's beliefs or hurt the girl. "I understand that you believe what you just said—"

"I knew you wouldn't believe me," Maria interjected, her voice tinged with frustration.

"That's not what I said," Carrie clarified.

"But that's what you meant. Whether you believe it or not, Ms. Vera's in trouble, and she needs help."

"I'll try to get her to talk to someone, but we can't force her to seek professional help—"

"She doesn't need *that* kind of help."

Carrie leaned back, crossing her hands on the desk. "I'm not sure what you want from me, Maria.

What you're saying is...well, it's just..." She let out a sigh. "It's challenging for me to accept."

Frustration flared in Maria's eyes. "I thought you were Ms. Vera's friend."

"Of course I am."

"Then help me to help *her*."

"Elena's obviously going through something, and I'm sure she just needs time to figure things out and get right with whatever she's facing. Adults can be complicated, Maria, and sometimes they are going through other things we don't know about that may not affect them right away but weigh on them until they just finally break down. I don't expect you—"

"Because I'm seventeen, I won't understand? Why do adults always think teens don't understand 'adult' problems? We deal with complicated shit every day that you don't even know about. We understand more than you know. Ms. Vera is in some real bad trouble, the kind *you* don't under-stand or don't want to because you don't believe."

Carrie was moved by Maria's words, respecting the courage it took to come and share something she knew would probably be dismissed as childish fantasy or ignorance.

"You're right. I shouldn't dismiss your feelings and your beliefs, whether I believe or not. I don't know what's wrong with Elena because she's shut me out, but I know that she is *not* herself. I'm not sure how you think you can help her, but I believe you think you can. I'm going to trust you because I do care about Elena. She's like family to me."

"Thank you, Ms. Drake," Maria said, rising from her seat and bending to hug Carrie. "So what are we going to do?"

"For starters, we're going to her apartment because she's obviously not taking my phone calls." Carrie remembered the last call and decided she needed to see Elena in person because her best friend was not okay. "But not today. Let's give her one more night to cool off. We'll go tomorrow after school."

NINE

Carrie's car was still in the shop, and there was no way she'd be caught dead riding public transportation of any variety, so she ordered a Lyft, which picked them up from the faculty parking lot after school the following day. It was Maria's first experience with a rideshare, which initially struck Carrie as amusing until she recognized her growing disconnect from her students and their daily struggles.

Elena's building was a three-story rehab, with one condo on each floor. Situated on a semi-quiet side street, the building had limited permit-only parking, which wouldn't be a problem since they arrived in a rideshare and didn't need to park. Carrie knew the four-digit security code to buzz them inside. Elena had shared it with her for the nights when they used to gather for girls' nights, binging on *Game of Thrones* or *Yellowjackets*, indulging in thick slices of stuffed pizza and spicy chicken wings (then regretting the copious amounts of carbs the next day). Those gatherings had become rare, since Elena and Natalie had ended their relationship.

Carrie and Maria entered the lobby of the building and ascended the stairs slowly (no elevator here). Carrie mentally rehearsed what they would say when Elena opened the door. Every scenario that played through her mind ended with Elena slamming the door in their faces. Of course, there was the possibility she wouldn't even open the door, given how angry Elena was with her (and rightly so).

Finally, they reached the third-floor landing, both exchanging hesitant glances before facing Elena's door. Carrie broke the silence. "Let me do the talking."

Maria raised an eyebrow. "Are you sure that's a good idea? She's pissed at you."

"She is, but I doubt she'd be any happier to see you on her doorstep."

"Yeah, she'll be mad you brought me here. Now she'll be double pissed at you."

Carrie sighed, scratching her left wrist, a nervous

habit when she was stressed. "You're making me regret this already."

Maria knocked on the door, three gentle raps. After nearly a minute of silence, Carrie knocked more insistently.

"Are you trying to scare her?" Maria asked. "That's how the cops knock on doors."

Carrie chuckled. "I won't ask how you know that."

"I've seen it on TV." Maria looked hurt. "Do you think I'm a thug or something because I'm Latina?"

Carrie looked at Maria, initially taking her seriously until she noticed the smirk on her face. "You had me going there for a second, girl."

Both of them jumped as the door was snatched open. Elena stood there, dressed in baggy gray joggers and an oversized Northside Chicago Prep T-shirt. Her hair was pulled back into a messy ponytail, and deep purplish circles under her eyes revealed her lack of sleep.

"What are you doing here?" Elena asked. She looked drained, exhausted.

"We came by to check on you," Carrie replied.

"We're both worried," Maria added.

Elena's hand slipped off the doorknob, as if she were too weak to hold it any longer. "Come in, I guess," she mumbled, then moved to the kitchen island and sat on a stool.

Carrie and Maria exchanged glances again, then entered and closed the door behind them. They took seats across from Elena, who leaned forward with her chin resting on her hands.

"Were you sleeping, El?" Carrie asked. She glanced at her watch. "It's like four in the afternoon."

"I've been having trouble sleeping, actually."

"I'll make some coffee," Maria offered. She got up and started rummaging through the unfamiliar kitchen cabinets in search of coffee grounds and filters.

"You look exhausted," Carrie said.

"I haven't slept in like twenty-four hours, maybe longer. What is today?"

"Jesus, El, it's Friday. What is wrong with you?"

"I don't know what's wrong with me," Elena admitted. "I'm losing my mind maybe. I'm seeing things that I know aren't there. I keep having the same nightmare every night, and I've got these"— she raised her shirt, revealing several large bruises on her left flank and lower back—"and I don't even know how I got them."

Maria gasped and covered her mouth. Carrie

stood and walked over for a closer look. "Maria, turn on the light. The switch is by the door."

Examining the fresh bruises, Carrie gently prodded Elena's flank and pulled away when she gasped.

"*Oough*, that hurts!"

Pulling Elena's shirt back down, Carrie stood up. She gripped Elena's face between both hands and turned her friend's face and locked eyes with her. "Elena, who did this to you?"

Elena stared directly back at her, silent for a moment. Then she whispered, "*La vieja malvada.*"

"What?"

"The evil old woman," Maria translated.

"Who is that, El? Who is she?"

"I've seen her," Maria whispered.

Carrie turned to Maria, bewildered. "You've seen who? What are you both talking about?"

Maria said, "I saw her in my dream." To Elena, she said, "*Pero era tu sueño!*" ("*But it was your dream!*")

"English, please," Carrie said.

Elena stood and moved closer to Maria, their faces just inches apart. "Tell me," she said, gripping Maria's arms.

"What's happening?" Carrie was utterly confused, felt like she was missing a big piece of the puzzle and everyone but her could see the finished picture. "Maria, what did you say?"

"I saw the evil woman in my dream, but it was *her* dream," Maria explained, pointing at Elena, her eyes never leaving her teacher. "You were on a ladder, looking into the dark place. You saw *la vieja malvada* in the corner, illuminated by the flashlight. She attacked you, knocked you down. She climbed on top of you, and the snakes without eyes came out of her mouth and went into yours. Then she saw me. She came for me, too. She did this."

Maria tugged down the neck of her shirt, revealing the shallow scratches on her shoulder. Elena gasped and covered her mouth.

Carrie stepped back with her hands outstretched. "Hold on, timeout. We need to take a big step back because I am all kinds of lost here." She looked at Maria. "You're saying you had a dream about Elena being attacked by an old woman, and in the dream, the old woman attacked you, too, and you woke up with scratches?"

Maria nodded. Her jaw was set, and her eyes were serious.

"It wasn't a dream," Elena said to Maria. "It was *real*."

TEN

THEY MIGRATED TO THE LIVING ROOM WHERE ELENA settled into her favorite chair, legs folded beneath her. Maria took charge of pouring coffee, then joined Carrie on the sofa. As they gathered around, they absorbed Elena's unsettling narrative—one that began with her recurring nightmare and spiraled into a series of nightmarish events: silver eyes lurking in the closet upon waking, hallucinations at Starbucks where everyone froze in a macabre flash mob, the eerie classroom incident that ended in her forced medical leave, and the inexplicable lost hours she'd experienced, culminating in a horrifying episode in the attic that somehow spilled into Maria's dream. Elena's account reached its crescendo as she recounted her memory of being attacked by the sinister *vieja malvada* just before losing consciousness.

Carrie turned toward Maria on the sofa, seeking clarification. "So you dreamed all this about Elena in the attic and this...*vieja*..." She trailed off, trying to find the word.

"*Malvada*. Evil," Maria helped her.

"Yes, *vieja malvada*. She attacked you and left those scratches? In the dream?"

Maria nodded vigorously, her hands moving as fast as she spoke. "She was on top of Ms. Vera—"

"Please, just call me Elena," Elena interjected.

"—and she had these snakes that had no eyes coming out of her mouth—I think they are her tongue—and they went into Ms. Vera's mouth and her throat, and they were choking her, and I screamed in my mind because I couldn't speak, couldn't make sounds in the dream, but *la vieja malvada* somehow heard me, like she was in my head or something because she looked up at me like she became aware of me suddenly, and then she lunged at me with her claws, and then...and then...I woke up screaming in my bed. My shoulder hurt like it was on fire, and I ran into the bathroom, and when I looked at it in the mirror, I saw the scratches."

"Are you sure you maybe didn't scratch your-self?" Carrie wondered.

Maria shook her head. "I thought the same thing at first, because what happened in the dream that couldn't be real, right? That just can't happen. But look at them." She pulled down the collar of her shirt so that Carrie could get another look.

"They're too big and too wide for you to have done that yourself," Carrie confirmed.

Facing Elena, Carrie said, "Does what Maria saw match your dream?"

"I *wasn't* dreaming, Carrie. I was awake. But what she says is what I experienced...at least until I blacked out," Elena said. She shifted in her chair and set her feet on the floor. "I didn't see the tongue-snake-thingy. Not then at least, but I did see it in my nightmare. The one when *la vieja malvada* attacked me as a girl. She...pushed the snake-tongues down my throat, and that's where I always wake, the same thing every night."

An uncomfortable silence fell over the room, like a shroud enveloping their collective unease. The sinister occurrences described by Elena, somehow brought to life in Maria's dream, left them suspended in a realm of inexplicable horrors and momentarily speechless.

"There's more you should know," Elena said finally, her eyes shifting between her friend and student.

"God, I'm not sure I want to know more," Carrie said.

Maria placed a hand on Carrie's arm. "We have to know."

Carrie put her hand over Maria's. "I know, but I'm still trying to process what I just heard." To Elena, she said, "Tell us, El. We're here for you."

Elena began to recount the horrors she'd faced over the last few days. She described an incident involving the bathroom mirror, where her reflection distorted and morphed into the malevolent face of *la vieja malvada* before she lunged out of the mirror, frightening Elena so badly, she jumped backward, tripped up on the lip of the tub, and hit her head on the shower wall. She told of a perplexing dinner that had suddenly transformed the microwaved chicken nuggets she'd nuked into grotesque eyeballs, which oozed blood instead of barbecue sauce when she bit into one, sickening her, forcing her to run for the kitchen, where she vomited.

"I haven't slept for I don't know how long now, because every time I start to doze, I hear a chorus of

voices getting louder and louder, chanting something over and over again...”

“That's what I heard the other day when I called
you,” Carrie said.

“What do you mean?”

Carrie looked uncomfortable. “When I called
you that night, after Mike sent you home. I tried to
apologize, but you said some mean things and then
your voice was drowned out by the chanting. It got
louder and louder, and then there was a horrible
screeching sound that made me drop the phone, and
when I picked it up, the call was disconnected.”

Elena looked confused. “Care, I never picked up
your call. I was angry, I felt betrayed, and every time
you called, it made me furious all over again, so I
never answered the phone.”

“But I heard your voice. It was you. I talked to
you a million times, and I know what you sound like.
Even when you're pissed.”

“It wasn't me,” Elena insisted.

“O-kay,” Carrie said. “This is...this is just getting
too fucking bizarre. I feel like we're all in a really
messed-up episode of *Black Mirror*.”

Elena stood up suddenly. “It gets worse, I'm
afraid. Come with me.”

There was one more thing Elena felt compelled

to share with them, but she had to *show* them the eerie discovery in her bedroom closet. Leading them down the narrow hallway and into her bedroom, she swung open the closet door and revealed the infamous hatch leading to the attic. She directed their gaze to the unnerving ominous black mold, roughly the size and shape of a cantaloupe, which spread from the right corner of the hatch.

Elena's voice trembled as she explained, "This wasn't here two nights ago, and last night, it was a spot the size of a quarter."

"It's spreading fast," Maria stated the obvious.

The room seemed to grow colder, and an unsettling dread hung heavily in the air and upon their shoulders.

ELEVEN

Back in the living room they gathered again, settling into the same places on the sofa and chair as before Elena showed them the inexplicable black mold forming along the attic hatch. None of them knew what to make of the growth, and it was frightening to think how quickly it spread. Carrie's first suggestion was that Elena should contact a specialist to take samples of the fungus—if that's even what it was—for testing and remediation, but who could they call about supernatural mold? They'd have to have *someone* look at the growth, because they couldn't just leave it or ignore it and hope it would go away. And at the rate of spread, it would soon overwhelm the entire closet and make its way into the bedroom, possibly down the walls until it enshrouded Elena like a fuzzy, viscous black cocoon. Carrie shuddered to think what would eventually emerge...

Carrie turned to Maria, her eyes wide with a mix of fear and curiosity, and asked, "Maria, what do you think we can do to help Elena in this...situation? You said you thought you could help."

Maria nodded. She'd grown up hearing tales of malevolent entities from her family, stories passed down through generations that spoke of spirits capable of possessing the living and inflicting hallucinations, bizarre behaviors, compulsions, and even self-harm.

"I believe Ms. Vera may be haunted by an evil entity," Maria said. "It can attach itself to a person, causing all these horrors she's been experiencing. My family, they believe in these things, and my mother once told me about a woman—a *curandera* (healer)—skilled in a ritual called *La Limpia* (spiritual cleansing). The *curandera* and cleansing ritual are believed to be capable of removing an entity and its influence from the possessed."

As Maria spoke, both women exchanged glances filled with a mixture of apprehension and disbelief. Maria sensed their skepticism and quickly added, "I know it sounds superstitious and even ridiculous to you, but in our culture, we hold strong beliefs in these practices and have for centuries. Ms. Vera, you're originally from Ecuador, right? Haven't you heard similar stories?"

Elena's brow furrowed. "I left Ecuador when I was very young, and my mother never shared stories like that. She believed that even discussing evil such as you describe was an invitation that could open the door to let it in."

"We don't doubt you, Maria," Carrie assured her. "Not after what Elena has seen, has experienced... not to mention the black shit on the ceiling." She paused a moment, considering, then asked, "Can you arrange for the *curandera* to see Elena? To perform the ritual you mention?"

Maria perked up. "Yes! I'll contact her tomorrow and talk to her. I'm sure she'll help."

Carried looked at Elena and smiled. "That sounds promising, doesn't it, El?"

Elena returned the smile, though her eyes betrayed her expression. "Yes, it does. Thank you both. I've been feeling so...isolated and alone. I felt like I was losing my mind. I don't know what I would have done without you both."

Carrie got up and went to Elena, knelt beside the chair where she sat. She took her hands. "You're not alone. I'm here for you." She glanced at Maria and reached out a hand. "We're here for you."

Maria joined them, taking Carrie's hand and flanking Elena. "You're going to get through this, Ms. Vera. You're so strong, but everyone needs help sometimes, and you can lean on us."

A very emotional Elena put an arm around Maria's shoulder and pulled her close. "You really need to call me Elena," she said. "Save the Ms. Vera stuff for the classroom."

Maria laughed. "I'll try, but no promises. Elena."

The hours passed, and they stayed with Elena, offering comfort and reassurance. They watched episodes of *New Girl*. (Maria had never seen the show before and was immediately smitten with Jess and the gang.) As the hour grew late, Maria asked if she and Carrie should spend the night, to watch over Elena and provide support, but Elena was adamant that they should leave. She feared that whatever was afflicting her might somehow latch onto them, and she couldn't bear the thought of causing harm to her friends. Carrie attempted to get Elena to come stay at her house then, but Elena refused, concerned that whatever haunted her would follow her, putting Carrie in danger.

"I'm not sure that's how it works," Carrie said, "but I'm going to respect your wishes."

As midnight approached, they finally embraced Elena and said their goodbyes. Maria, at the door, took Elena's hand and placed a simple redwood rosary into her palm. "Keep this by your bedside. It was blessed by the cardinal at my confirmation. It may offer some protection."

Elena nodded gratefully, clutching the rosary in her hand. "Thank you," she whispered, hugging Maria tightly.

"See you tomorrow, babe," Carrie said, and she hugged Elena again.

Elena managed a faint smile, her voice trembling with emotion. "Be safe, you two."

"I'll take care of your car," Carrie assured her, holding up the key fob. "I promise."

They waited for Elena to close and lock the door, then the two of them made their way down the three flights of stairs. Outside, the evening was brisk. The street was well-lit by evenly spaced streetlamps. Elena's Honda was parked half a block down, and Carrie and Maria locked arms, taking in the brisk air as they walked.

"Do you really think the *curandera*—man, that

just sounds weird coming out of my mouth—can help?" Carrie asked.

Maria looked at Carrie, her eyes reflecting uncertainty that she didn't show back in Elena's condo when she said she'd make the arrangements. "I don't know, but we have to try, right?"

"Absolutely," Carrie affirmed.

In the car, Carrie made some adjustments to the driver's seat and mirrors, because Elena was a few inches shorter. As the engine roared to life, she turned on the heater, providing a much-needed warmth after the short stroll in the sharp night air. They set off for Maria's home, passing the next twenty minutes mostly in silence, each lost in her thoughts about Elena. When they arrived at Maria's place, Carrie broke the silence.

"You're a brave girl," she praised Maria, her admiration evident in her eyes.

Maria blushed, didn't know what to say. She opened the car door, got out, then leaned in. "And you're a good friend to Ms. Vera."

Carrie shrugged. "I'm getting better at it. And just so you know, we're friends, too, Maria."

Touched, Maria leaned further into the car, her knee on the passenger seat, and hugged Carrie affectionately. She planted a gentle kiss on Carrie's cheek and whispered, "Good night," before hurrying out, closing the door behind her, and dashing up the porch steps. Once inside, she locked the door and leaned back against it, a whirlwind of emotions surging within her.

Overwhelmed and yet inexplicably happy, Maria couldn't help but bask in the warmth of love and friendship that so suddenly came into her life and enveloped her. She tiptoed quietly to her room, mindful not to wake her mother, who would soon be rising for work in the next few hours. Stripping off her clothes, she exchanged them for a pair of jogging shorts and a comfortable T-shirt, not giving a thought to the scratches on her shoulder. As she crawled into her bed, the cool sheets provided a soothing contrast against her warm skin, sending a shiver down her spine. She pulled the blanket up over herself, rolled onto her left side, and soon fell into a dreamless sleep.

TWELVE

MARIA SPENT THE MORNING ARRANGING THE cleansing ritual. With help from her mother (after much pleading), she'd convinced the *curandera* the situation was urgent, and she agreed to see them later in the afternoon. Of course, Carrie wanted to go with them, but Maria told her that the *curandera* would not allow it but promised she and Elena would fill her in on all the details as soon as the ritual was complete. Carrie insisted on driving them and waiting outside in the car—"In case we have to make a quick getaway," she joked. They both knew that Carrie needed to be part of this in some way— they were a trio on this journey, for better or worse —and they accepted her chauffeur services.

They drove to the Pilsen neighborhood on the lower west side of Chicago, just a couple miles south of downtown. The historic neighborhood was rich in Latino culture, home to offbeat boutiques, hip eateries, and cool music venues standing alongside bodegas, panaderias, and family-owned restaurants serving authentic Mexican cuisine. Maria guided them to a place called *Mercado y Carniceria* near the busy intersection of 18th Street and Ashland Avenue. There was no parking lot or designated parking on the crowded block, so Carrie had to double park alongside other cars parked along the curb and drop them off near the front entrance.

"I'm going to drive around and see if I can find somewhere to park. Text me when you're out, and I'll come get you," Carrie said. Maria and Elena could tell she was stressed, though she tried to hide the tension in her voice. She was not used to driving in the busy inner-city traffic.

After Carrie pulled away, Elena and Maria stood in front of the small market. The street was busy this time of day, and the traffic sounds were constant. People moved quickly in both directions along the sidewalks, which were teeming with food carts, racks of clothing in front of cramped clothing shops, and tables filled with colorful and skillfully crafted handmade items.

"This is the place?" Elena asked.

Maria nodded. "Come on."

Once inside, Maria took Elena's hand and led her through the market, past crowded grocery aisles stocked with Mexican candies and authentic food items, and through a door beside the meat counter —where chunks of carnitas, carne seca, tamales, menudo, and other traditional food were displayed behind glass or atop the counter—to the back room where Rocio, the owner and resident *curandera* was waiting for them.

Rocio was a short, stocky woman in her late sixties with long black hair streaked with strands of fine silver pulled back into a severe ponytail. She wore a maroon smock with the store logo on the left breast over a dark blue shirt. She was a stern-looking woman with dark, kind eyes. She spoke with an accent, though she'd been in the United States since she was just a young girl.

"Come, come inside," she told them, waving them into the stock room.

They followed her across the stockroom—where men and women were hard at work unloading trucks or sorting goods from within boxes and affixing prices—and into a small room that Elena thought must be Rocio's office. Rocio directed them to sit at the table at the center of the room.

Elena, her eyes wide and skin pale, glanced nervously around the cramped room, its walls adorned with crucifixes and herbs. "Is this...safe?" she stammered.

"Safe, *sí*," Rocio reassured, lighting candles that cast flickering shadows. "But not easy. *La Limpia* requires strength."

By dim candlelight, Rocio methodically prepared to perform the spiritual cleansing, meticulously arranging the tools of her trade on the table before them. Her hands moved with a graceful precision, each gesture practiced and steady, as if guided by an ancient wisdom passed down through generations.

Elena and Maria watched silently as Rocio placed a small clay bowl filled with smoldering sage leaves at one corner of the table. The pungent scent of burning sage filled the room, purifying the air and creating a thin veil of smoke that shimmered in the candlelight. She arranged an assortment of dried herbs, each with its own unique properties and symbolism. Maria recognized bundles of rosemary, lavender, and rue, all carefully tied with colorful threads. These herbs were believed to possess protective and purifying qualities, essential for banishing malevolent forces. Her grandmother kept neatly tied bundles in the drawer of her nightstand and in the kitchen.

Rocio placed a small vial of water at the center of the table, its contents shimmering in the candlelight. Maria knew the vial contained holy water, a potent weapon against evil spirits, capable of dispelling darkness and restoring purity. Surrounding the vial of holy water were various charms and trinkets—an intricately carved cross, a bundle of garlic cloves, and a silver amulet engraved with protective symbols. These objects served as symbols of faith and protection, strengthening the power of the ritual.

Elena gripped Maria's arm and looked into the girl's eyes for reassurance as Rocio began to pour a circle of salt around the table, then stood just outside the ring that now marked the boundaries of their sacred space. With a solemn expression, she began to chant in a hauntingly melodic voice, invoking the ancient spirits and seeking their aid in cleansing Elena's soul.

As Rocio chanted, she dipped a feather into the smoldering sage and gently fanned the fragrant smoke over Elena. The smoke enveloped Elena, its tendrils swirling around her like ethereal tendrils, penetrating her very essence. The candles on the altar flickered in response to Rocio's invocation, casting eerie shadows on the walls. The room seemed to come alive, as if it were a sentient entity bearing witness to the unfolding battle between light and darkness.

Rocio's chanting grew louder, her words imbued with an urgency that echoed through the room. Her movements became more deliberate as she continued to fan the sage smoke over Elena, her eyes locked onto Elena's strained expression. With each passing moment, the energy in the room grew more palpable, the sense of impending confrontation between good and evil becoming almost suffocating. Maria's heart raced, caught in the tense drama of the ritual, and a bead of sweat trickled down her temple.

As Rocio chanted and the energy crackled, that low, menacing growl erupted from the shadows, chilling Maria to the bone. It was as if the malevolent force lurking in Elena's soul had awakened, angered by the attempt to cleanse it.

Elena's breaths came in short gasps.

"What's happening?" she whispered to Maria, her voice trembling.

Ignoring the girl, Rocio pressed on, her voice unwavering, her faith unshaken. She knew the risks, and she was determined to see the ritual through to the end, no matter what horrors might be unleashed.

The room seemed to respond to the growing tension. The candles flickered wildly, casting macabre, shifting shapes on the walls that danced in time with the *curandera's* chants. The pungent scent of burning sage hung heavy in the air, mingling with the undertones of fear.

Elena, sitting in the center of the circle, was a portrait of torment as her face contorted in sudden agony as Rocio's chants intensified, as if the evil within her abruptly rebelled against the cleansing light. Beads of sweat glistened on her forehead, and her fingers clenched Maria's arm in a vice-like grip.

The temperature dropped suddenly, a cold gust extinguishing the candles. A deep, guttural growl reverberated through the darkness. Maria clutched Elena's hand, her own fear palpable.

"Rocio, what is that?" Maria's voice cracked with terror, her breath held in a tight grip, as the room's energy seemed to crescendo. The growl, now more pronounced, reverberated through the very bones of the room. The candles wavered, and the air chilled further, leaving Maria trembling.

Then the room's transformation from a haven of hope to a chamber of malevolence took a terrifying turn. Objects on the wooden table beside Rocio came to life with a demonic fury. Bottles of holy water, the bundles of herbs, and the protective charms levitated and spun like the cogs of some dark, unseen machinery. Maria's gasp was drowned out by the cacophonous chaos as the room itself seemed to convulse. Heavy wind tore through the closed room, creating a maelstrom of swirling dust and debris. The world inside seemed to have descended into madness.

The walls seemed to pulse, crucifixes trembling. A sinister laughter, alien and chilling, erupted from Elena's mouth.

Rocio pressed a talisman against Elena's forehead, her voice rising in a desperate plea. "By the light, I command you to leave!"

The room shook violently, objects crashing around them. Elena's scream, a mix of agony and fear, filled the air as blood trickled from her nose. "It hurts!" she cried.

Elena's body violently lifted off the chair, propelled by an unseen force, her hair whipping around her like the tentacles of a sea monster. Maria bolted from her seat, hands trembling and instinctively extending toward Elena, whose body was manipulated like a marionette by an evil puppeteer from hell.

With a deafening crash, Elena was violently thrown across the room, her body slamming into the wall with bone-crushing force. Maria's scream was swallowed by the maelstrom of chaos that raged around them. Rocio clung to her beliefs, chanting even louder now, the words flowing like a protective barrier against the malevolent force.

On the wooden table, the unseen presence carved words into the surface with wicked claws, leaving a permanent scar as a testament to its power. Sinister whispers and chilling laughter filled the room, drowning out Rocio's prayers. In a final act of desperation, Rocio crossed herself repeatedly, her voice shaking but unwavering. She implored the divine for intervention as the room descended further into the abyss.

Then, as abruptly as it had all begun, the room fell silent. The candles flickered back to a calm, steady flame. The herbs and trinkets lay still on the floor, their rebellion quelled. The Latin words etched into the table remained, a haunting reminder of the battle that had raged within these walls.

Maria, her heart racing with dread, darted to Elena's side. Elena was slumped against the wall, her body unnervingly still. Maria's hands trembled as she reached out, her voice quivering with terror. "Elena? Can you hear me?"

Elena's response was a mere murmur, her eyelids fluttering weakly. As her eyes opened, they were clouded with confusion and fear. "M-Maria?" Her voice was a frail whisper, laced with pain and disorientation.

Maria, fighting back her own rising panic, tried to sound reassuring, though her voice was laced with a palpable fear. "Yes, it's me. Can you stand?"

Elena struggled to her feet, her movements shaky and uncertain. She leaned heavily on Maria, her body racked with shivers. Each step was a battle, her legs barely supporting her weight.

Rocio turned to Maria, her face drained of color, and whispered harshly, "*Este mal está más allá de mí. Ha reclamado a Elena, y no la dejará ir. Debes irte ahora, y nunca debes regresar! Aquí ya no es Seguro.*" ("This evil is beyond me. It's claimed Elena, and it won't let go. You must leave now, and you must never return! It's not safe here anymore.")

Maria's pleas were frantic, her voice a desperate tremor. "*Rocío, por favor, tienes que ayudarla. No podemos dejarla así.*" ("Rocio, please, you have to help her. We can't leave her like this.")

Rocio, her demeanor hardened by fear and determination, frantically ushered them toward the side door that let out into the alley. "*¡Vete! Vete ya!*" ("Leave! Go now!")

She closed it firmly behind them, leaving Maria and Elena standing in the alley among the chilling shadows of the flanking buildings.

In the shadows of the alley, Elena's fragile composure shattered. Her body wracked with violent sobs, and she clung to Maria like a lifeline. Maria wrapped an arm around Elena, guiding her with gentle insistence. As they walked—each step felt like wading through a nightmare, the echoes of Rocio's warnings reverberating in their minds— Maria pulled out her phone and with trembling fingers typed a quick message to Carrie to pick them up. The text screen was a blur through her tears.

"Maria, I...I can't believe she just...threw us out

like that." Elena's voice broke, the words spilling out between ragged breaths.

Maria, her own fear a suffocating shroud around her, struggled to find words that could offer solace. "Elena, we're going to get through this, I promise," she whispered, her voice trembling as she fought to mask her terror. But her words felt hollow, lost in the overwhelming shadow of the unseen horror that had ensnared Elena.

Elena's response was a choked gasp, a sound of utter despair that cut through the night. "Maria, she...she couldn't help me. What am I going to do?" Her voice was a raw, frayed thread, barely holding together against the overwhelming panic.

Maria squeezed her hand, offering a meager comfort in the face of the inexplicable horror they had just witnessed. "I know, Elena, I know. Let's just get you home," she murmured.

As they reached the car, Carrie's alarmed expression only heightened the sense of unreality. The world outside their bubble of horror seemed oblivious, carrying on as if nothing had changed. Carrie's words, "What happened?" hit them like a physical blow, a stark reminder of their newfound isolation in a nightmare that only they had witnessed.

"Just take me home," Elena pleaded, her voice a

fragile whisper that carried the weight of their shattered reality.

The drive home was a silent, torturous journey. The city blurred past, uncaring and distant. Elena's quiet weeping, a haunting melody of despair, was the only sound that filled the car.

THIRTEEN

UPON RETURNING TO ELENA'S CONDO, SHE WENT directly to her room and closed the door behind her. After a few moments, Carrie and Maria knocked gently on the door and then went inside. The bathroom door was closed and the shower was running. Through the door, they heard Elena crying.

"I feel so bad for her," Maria said.

Carrie put a hand on the girl's shoulder. "I know, honey. So do I."

"Should one of us go in there?"

"No. Let's give her some time alone."

Maria hesitated. "Are you sure? After what she just went through..."

"I'm sure. Come on, let's make some tea."

They left the bedroom, closing the door. In the

kitchen, Carrie started the electric kettle while Maria set out a ceramic tea pot and added several peppermint tea bags. They sat at the island while they waited for the water to boil and the tea to steep.

"How are you doing?" Carrie asked.

"I'm fine," Maria responded quickly.

Carrie looked at the girl. It was obvious she was shaken up by whatever happened in the market, but she was putting on a brave face. She didn't want to pressure Maria, but she needed to know what transpired at the cleansing.

"I don't know what happened, but seeing how distressed El is, you must be feeling the same."

"It happened to her, not me," Maria said.

"But you were there. You...experienced it, too. Don't minimize that."

Maria got up and fetched the electric kettle. "It was pretty awful," she said as she poured hot water into the ceramic pot. She put the lid on so the tea could steep, then sat down again.

Reaching out for Maria's hand, Carrie asked, "Do you think you can tell me what happened in there?"

Grateful for the contact, Maria gently accepted Carrie's hand. It was warm and comforting. She nodded her head.

"Take your time."

After taking a moment to compose her thoughts, Maria recounted the frightening events—doing her best to accurately depict every detail, no matter how hard it was to describe the ordeal—ending with Rocio ushering them out into the alleyway behind the market.

Carrie listened, horrified and deeply heart-broken at what Elena and Maria both faced. The thought of a young woman having to witness such horror was unfathomable and brought tears to Carrie's eyes.

"I am so sorry you had to go through that. I should have gone in with her, not you," Carrie said.

"Rocio was my idea, my responsibility."

Carrie shook her head. "You're so amazing, Maria. Elena is so lucky to have you in her life. I'm so lucky, too."

"Are you trying to make me cry?" Maria asked, blotting the corners of her eyes with her knuckles. "Because it's working."

"Let it out, girl. Look at us, just a couple of badass chicks bawling our eyes out and sharing our feelings."

They both laughed a little and blotted at their eyes as they regained their composure.

After sipping tea, Carrie asked, "So what's next? This isn't over yet. How do we help Elena?"

"I don't know. But what I do know is Elena can't be alone. Rocio said the evil has a hold of her. The frequency of her dreams, the hallucinations, the way she lost time before going in the attic, whatever is happening is getting worse."

"She won't be alone. I'm going to take a week of sick time and couch surf here."

"That's a good idea. And I'll tell my mother I'm going to spend a few nights at my friend's house so I can help, you know, give you a break if you need it."

Surprisingly, Carrie did not object to Maria lying to her mother and spending the night. The fact was she was scared and unsure and had no idea what to do. The thought of having someone by her side was comforting. And Maria seemed to know more about the supernatural and was perhaps more equipped to handle the situation than she.

"I call the chair and ottoman," Maria said, bringing Carrie back to the moment.

"Oh, thank God," Carrie said in a rush of breath, "because my back can't handle sleeping in the upright position."

"Don't worry, I got you, Ms. D."

Standing up and stretching, Carrie said, "In the meantime, I'm starving. How does pizza sound?"

"Amazing!"

"El and I usually order from this local place, Father and Sons. Best pizza in the city."

"Oh, bold words. Do they have stuffed?"

"Of course they do," Carrie said. "It's not Chicago pizza if it ain't deep dish. Sausage, pepper, and onion good?"

"We are so sympatico," Maria said, also standing. "I'm going to check on Elena while you order."

Carrie nodded as she pulled out her iPhone and opened the Slice app, noting she was one more pizza order away from getting a free pizza. She'd use that later in the week.

Maria slipped down the short hallway and paused at the bedroom door. She put her ear to it, but there was only silence from the other side. She knocked gently and then turned the knob and opened the door slowly.

Elena was on the bed, curled up with the blanket pulled up under her chin. Damp heat emanated from the bathroom as the heat of the shower slowly dissipated. Standing beside her, Maria looked her over, an overwhelming sensation of love and adoration filled her, but also a deep sadness. The poor woman did not deserve what was happening to her, not any of it. Not one damn bit.

In the living room, Carrie sat on the sofa with her feet up under her. She looked over her shoulder as Maria approached. "The pie will be here in about forty-five minutes. In the meantime, care to binge watch *Peacekeeper* with me? The kids keep talking about it. They say it's funny as hell and has a great soundtrack for boomers."

Plopping down onto the chair and kicking her feet up onto the ottoman, Maria said, "John Cena? Yum. I'm in."

They watched the first two episodes—the kids were right, it was damn funny, but also had a good plot and a good mix of action and drama—before the pizza arrived. Maria popped the tabs on two cans of Diet Coke while Carrie used a pie spatula to finagle two gooey, dripping slices of deep dish onto each of their plates.

They ate in the living room so they could continue watching television. Maria looked down at the plate on the ottoman and declared, "No way I can eat two."

"You won't know until you try," Carrie said as she speared one of her slices with a fork and sawed into it with a knife. Deep dish wasn't a dainty pie, and you didn't just pick it up in your hands and eat it.

"Challenge accepted."

After the fourth episode, Maria stood up and took her plate to the kitchen where she added her remaining slice of pizza—she failed the challenge hard—into the greasy box on the island. Carrie managed to finish both of her slices, but her stomach felt swollen.

"I got the dishes," Carrie said, taking the plate from Maria and dropping it and her own into the sink before running the hot water.

"I'll check on El."

Elena was still asleep, though she'd pushed aside her blankets and now laid on her stomach facing the windows. Her face glistened with sweat and her hair stuck to her forehead and neck. Maria smoothed Elena's hair back gently and then placed the back of her wrist against her forehead. She was warm but not feverish.

While Carrie finished up the dishes, Maria put away the leftover pizza and used Clorox wipes to swab the island and then to clean up the coffee table in the living room. Carrie located spare blankets in the hall closet and tossed one to Maria.

"Bed time, kid. It's a school night."

"Okay, Mom," Maria quipped, caught the blanket onehanded, and nestled into the chair. It was oversized and quite roomy, especially under her petite body. She snuggled up against a throw pillow, pulled the blanket up to her neck, and closed her eyes.

"Good night, Carrie."

"Night," Carrie said and snapped off the lamp.

They both quickly fell asleep, emotionally and physically exhausted by the events and stress of the day. Maria woke a few hours later, feeling a bit warm and an urge to pee. The room was dark, but illumination from the streetlamps filtered through the blinds. Elena stood in front of the sofa, staring intently at Carrie, who lay facing the back of the sofa, no doubt to avoid the light from outside. Maria watched her for nearly two minutes, her body swaying gently and her gaze remaining fixed on Carrie.

"Elena?" Maria whispered, her voice too soft to elicit a response. She called out Elena's name again, this time loud enough to wake Carrie, who groggily craned her neck to look over her shoulder.

"Jesus!" she yelped when she saw Elena and quickly maneuvered down and away and sat upright. She gathered herself after a moment, though her heart continued to ram in her chest. "Elena, what are you doing standing there?"

Elena did not respond. Carrie called her name again, but she still didn't respond, remained in the same position, rocking slightly back and forth, her eyes fixated on the spot where Carrie's head had been.

Freaked out by Elena's strange behavior, Carrie pushed off the blanket and slowly got up from the sofa, carefully skirting around Elena, and when she was passed her, she took a couple of quick steps away from her entranced friend. Maria was already out of her chair, standing beside Carrie, gripping her arm like a child afraid of getting lost at the mall.

"What the fuck?" Maria whispered.

Carrie tentatively stepped forward—pulling away from Maria's death grip—and placed each of her hands on Elena's shoulders. She shook her gently, softly speaking her name, like a mother waking her daughter for school. Elena did not respond.

Fear bloomed in Carrie's belly, the warmth of it spreading across her insides like a shot of bourbon. Stepping to the side, looking at the other woman's profile, Carrie took a breath before she yelled, "Elena!" and clapped her hands loudly.

Finally, Elena blinked several times, then turned her head slowly—her body remained rooted, and only her head swiveled as if she were an owl. Her eyes focused on Carrie for a few seconds, then shifted to Maria, who stared back uncomfortably. Elena's eyes locked on Maria's for nearly thirty seconds, her face blank but her gaze intense.

Maria felt completely chilled inside. The way Elena looked at her was creepy, like it wasn't even her teacher staring at her, but rather a predator sizing up prey. Her fear was palpable, and sensing it, Carrie shook Elena's shoulders again, much harder than previously, drawing her attention from Maria.

"Elena, what's wrong with you? What are you doing?"

In the dark room, Elena's eyes seemed devoid, as was her expression. She let out a soft gasp that smelled of sulfur, a foul smell that rocked Carrie back on her heels. A hissing sigh escaped her that rose in tempo until it sounded like a creaking door in desperate need of oil. Elena turned away, rotating on the heel of her left foot like a soldier executing an about-face, and walked back to her room, the sound tapering off as she went.

"What the *fuck* was that?" Carrie hissed when Elena was out of their sightline.

Maria shook her head, at a loss for words. Her face was pale, and she was visibly shaken. It was as if they'd been in the room with a complete stranger, and all sorts of internal alarms—*stranger danger!*—were sounding inside her head.

Carrie, seeing Maria's distress, went to her and hugged her. "We're fine, Elena's fine."

"No," Maria said. Her body tensed, and she leaned away from Carrie's embrace. "That wasn't Elena. That was something...*pura maldad* (pure evil). Didn't you feel it?"

Carrie hesitated a moment but then nodded her head. There was definitely an overwhelming sense of malevolent oppression she'd felt, a profound coldness, a dark emptiness—hell, she didn't know how else to describe what she'd felt in Elena's presence.

She didn't say it aloud, because she didn't want to frighten Maria any more than she clearly was, but Carrie couldn't help but wonder what might have happened if Maria hadn't woken to find Elena—*no, not Elena, something else, pura maldad*—standing over her. She shuddered when she wondered how long Elena had been standing over her before Maria woke.

Did she really believe Elena would have hurt

her? But the woman that stood in front of her wasn't entirely Elena, no, not Elena at all.

"Should we...I don't know, maybe check on her?" Maria asked.

"No!" Carrie shook her head, terrified of the idea of either of them putting themselves in the same room with the malevolent presence. "I don't think we should go in there. Not tonight, anyway."

"What if..."

"There's nothing we could do for her if...something's taken her. We have no idea what the fuck to do against an evil entity. We can't take that risk because we have to find someone who knows how to help Elena. To fight this thing. Do you know anyone else who can help? Someone else like Rocio?"

"No, she's all I know."

"Maybe we should go to the church? Right? Don't they do stuff like this?"

"I don't think they will help," Maria said. "The church doesn't believe in possession anymore. They'll want to send her to the hospital, to a psychiatrist to rule out mental illness, and even then, no guarantee they'd do anything about it."

Carrie considered this. Reluctantly, she said, "Maybe that's best. Let the professionals assess her and see what they recommend—"

"No fucking way—"

"Language, kid!"

"—we're doing that. They'd just think she's crazy or delusional and shoot her full of drugs and lock her in some room *where she'll be alone with that evil!*"

"That's a bit dramatic," Carrie said, but she knew Maria was right. "Look, maybe we're jumping the gun here. Maybe she was just sleepwalking. I saw a television show once where a man drove to a supermarket and brought the groceries to his mother's house and cooked a steak while asleep."

"Are you being serious right now?" Maria asked. "You were here, weren't you? You just saw what happened, and you know Elena was *not* sleepwalking. She was *possessed!*"

Carrie sat on one of the stools at the kitchen island before her legs gave out and she crashed to the floor. She put her head in her hands and squeezed at her temples. She felt completely drained, both mentally and physically, and utterly out of her element.

While she massaged her throbbing temples, she said, "I don't know what else to say or do. I'm not equipped to handle this crazy, fucked-up situation. I'm trying my best here."

Maria hugged Carrie from behind, resting her

head on Carrie's back. This was not a time for them to be divided. No, this was a time for them to lean on each other, to lift each other, support each other.

"I'm sorry," Maria said, feeling the slight rise and fall with each breath Carrie took. "I'm being such an ass right now."

"No, you're right," Carrie said. Her eyes felt so heavy that keeping them open was a chore. "You're the only one talking sense right now. We definitely can't let the psycho doctors take her."

"That's not gonna happen."

Carrie sat up and turned on the stool so she faced Maria. "We have to protect her. We need to figure out how. Any ideas?"

Maria puckered her lips and nodded. "I think I do."

"Want to share?"

"I'm going back to see Rocio. I may not know anyone else who can help, but I'm sure she does. She's part of the community that believes in all this shit; she has to know someone who can help, even if she can't."

"I should come with you. Strength in numbers, right?"

Maria shook her head. "We can't leave Elena

alone. You don't know Rocio or speak the language, so this has to be on me."

"Fair enough," Carrie said. As an afterthought, she asked, "Hey, do you even have a driver's license?"

"I do, got it last year. I don't have a car, though, so..."

Carrie stood up and grabbed her jacket from the coatrack beside the door. She dug Elena's car keys out of the pocket and held them out to Maria.

"I got you covered," she said, dropping the keys into Maria's awaiting hand.

Maria checked the clock on the microwave. It was just a bit after four. "I'll wait a few more hours, though. I think the market opens at nine."

"Okay. In the meantime, get some sleep. I'll keep watch, just in case..."

Maria didn't think she'd be able to sleep, but as soon as she fell into the comfortable chair and wrapped the blanket around her like a poncho, she was fast asleep.

Fourteen

Maria was exhausted and hated leaving Carrie on her own with Elena, but it was necessary. Elena was still asleep when she left the condo around eight-thirty. Carrie hugged her and told her to be careful. Half an hour later, she pulled into the alley beside the mercado where Rocio had banished them yesterday, pushing them out of her back room like they were lepers.

To both her and Elena, the situation felt deeply unsettling. Rocio's actions, far from honorable, left Maria with a lingering bitterness. She felt a profound sense of betrayal by a woman who had been deeply respected and held in high regard as a healer, not just by her and her family, but by the entire community as well.

Two unmarked refrigerated trucks were parked in front of the two large bay doors where men were removing boxes from the trucks and stacking them on dollies. Maria went around them, white knuckling the steering wheel as she navigated the narrow space between them and the building on the opposite side of the alley and parked near the side entrance.

Maria exited the car, careful to lock the doors—this was a less-than-savory neighborhood and the last thing she needed was for someone to steal Elena's car—and walked through the loading area. She passed several of Rocio's workers as she moved through the receiving dock, sure that one of them would call out that she shouldn't be here, but all of them focused on their work and none of them paid her any attention.

She climbed a few steps from the delivery area to the main platform and noticed Rocio discussing her order with a man in blue work clothes. Maria stopped where Rocio could see her and waited. Catching Rocio's attention, she raised a hand in a tentative greeting. Rocio quickly finished her conversation with the man who she then waved off.

Clasping the front of her sweater closed over her large bosom, Rocio crossed the floor. When she was several feet away, Maria said, "*Lo siento, sé que me pediste que no volviera—*" ("I'm sorry, I know you asked me not to come back—") but Rocio waved her words away.

"*No, no, no es necesario. Por favor, ven conmigo.*" ("No, no, not necessary. Please, come with me.")

Taking Maria's arm in her own, Rocio led the way to the back room, where less than twenty-four hours ago she'd performed the botched cleansing and Elena was assaulted by an unseen entity. Rocio had cleaned up since, sweeping up the broken glass and returning the frames and trinkets that had whirled around the room in the wake of an unseen force to their previous locations. There was no trace of the malevolence that raged within these walls.

Closing the door behind them, Rocio released Maria's arm and clasped her hands in front of her. In her heavily accented English, Rocio said, "I should apologize. I'm ashamed of my actions. I am embarrassed." She crossed herself before continuing. "*El demonio* is extremely powerful, stronger than any I have seen. This evil is pure and cannot be cleansed."

"There must be something, Rocio, someone who can help," Maria pleaded, grabbing Rocio's hands. "Please, I beg you."

Rocio stood silent, considering the girl's plea.

Her hands throbbed in Maria's desperate grip. After a moment, she closed her eyes and sighed. When she opened her eyes, she said, "There is someone who may be able to help... His name is Tomas."

"*¿Quién es ese Tomás? ¿Cómo puedo encontrarlo?*" ("Who is this Tomas? How can I find him?") A glimmer of hope lit in Maria's eyes.

Motioning for Maria to sit at the table, Rocio sat across from her, clasping her own hands in front of her. Her brown eyes stared directly at Maria, and in a serious tone, she said, "Tomas was a priest... *pero fue excomulgado.*" ("...but he was excommunicated.")

"Why? What happened?"

Reverting to Spanish, Rocio explained, "*Tomás no tenía permiso de la iglesia para realizar el ritual.*" ("Tomas did not have permission from the church to perform the ritual.")

"So they cast him out?"

Rocio looked into Maria's eyes. "A young boy died in the *exorcismo.*" She crossed herself again. "He was banished," she continued and lifted both hands before her, palms down, and slowly rotated them outward in a deliberate, sweeping motion. Her fingers splayed wide, as if shedding invisible droplets, the gesture deliberate and final, a clear disavowal and a resignation that severed ties.

"That's horrible," Maria said. It was always tragic when a young child was lost. In Chicago, kids died all the time, most because of senseless gun violence or domestic abuse. The thought of a child's fate being sealed in such a grim way weighed heavily on her. She turned her attention back to Rocio and asked, "What happened to Tomas afterward?"

"*Él todavía hace la obra de Dios pero no para la iglesia. Dirige un banco de alimentos y un refugio en Pilsen y hace lo que puede para ayudar a la comunidad a través de la caridad*")." ("He still does God's work but not for the church. He runs a food pantry and shelter in Pilsen and does what he can to help the community through charity.")

"Please tell me how to find him. I must go to him."

Rocio took a deep breath. "I will tell you how to find him, but you must prepare yourself. The boy's death haunts him, and he can't let go of the past," she said. She leaned forward and grabbed Maria's hand. "He will tell you he will not help. But you *must* convince him. The evil grows stronger every second, and once it reaches full power, there will be no help for her."

"How can I convince him?"

Rocio released Maria's hand and grasped the

tablecloth between both fists and pulled it back, revealing the Latin words gouged deeply into the surface.

Rocio said, "*Muéstrale eso a Tomas. Cuéntale lo que pasó aquí, lo que le está pasando a tu amigo. Y reza para que te ayude.*" ("Show that to Tomas. Tell him what happened here, what's happening to your friend. And pray that he will help.")

Maria stared at the scarred tabletop for a long moment—remembering the terror that clenched in her belly as the letters were gouged into the wood before her eyes—before taking out her phone. She opened the camera app and snapped several photos of the words. She had no idea what they meant, but the very sight of them chilled her.

FIFTEEN

MARIA'S DRIVE TO THE FOOD PANTRY WAS A BLUR OF traffic lights. She recounted her conversation with Rocio and rehearsed what she might say to the priest. Although Rocio was convinced he would not help willingly, Maria was convinced he would after hearing the horrors Elena experienced. How could he not? He might not be with the church, but at heart he was still a man of the cloth, a man of deep faith.

She parked in front of the two-story building where a mom-and-pop bodega once thrived before COVID, but eventually, like most of the small businesses on this stretch of Ashland Avenue, closed their doors when they could no longer make their rent payments due to severe decline in business.

Most of the other buildings were shuddered and abandoned, with FOR SALE signs plastered across their soaped or papered windows. The local archdiocese purchased the property and had established the food pantry in an attempt to help the growing number of impoverished in the area and to help aide the Venezuelan migrants that flooded into Chicago.

Stepping inside, Maria immediately spotted Tomas orchestrating the day's operations with a gentle authority, directing volunteers with a blend of kindness and efficiency. The sight of him, so grounded and serene, momentarily bolstered her hope. She approached him hesitantly, interrupting his conversation with a volunteer.

"Father Tomas?" Her voice was firmer than she felt.

"It's just Tomas these days," he said, turning to her, his expression open and welcoming until he saw the urgency in her eyes.

"I need to talk to you. Please. It's important."

With a nod of understanding, he placed a hand on the volunteer's shoulder and said, "Excuse me, Esme."

"Of course," Esme said. She made brief eye contact with Maria, then bowed her head slightly before she moved off to assist patrons.

Tomas clasped his hands in front of him. "Please, follow me," he said, turning gracefully upon his heel. He led Maria through the organized chaos—never turning to see if she followed—to a small office tucked away in the back. The room, crowded with books, icons, and the soft glow of candles, felt like a retreat—a reflection of a life devoted to others yet marked by the echoes of past regrets.

Tomas sat behind a small desk and motioned for Maria to sit in one of two chairs opposite him. Crossing his hands on the desk, he said, "You know my name, but I am afraid I do not know yours."

"Maria. It's nice to meet you," she said, offering her hand.

Tomas leaned forward, accepting her hand.

"Do I know you from the community?"

"We have a mutual friend. Rocio Aroca."

Tomas smiled. "Rocio...she is a good woman and friend to the community."

"She is," Maria agreed.

"You said you had something urgent to discuss..."

Maria leaned forward, gripping the edge of the desk. "Rocio sent me to you. She said you could help my friend."

"How can I help?"

Maria paused a moment, collecting herself before she finally recounted Elena's ordeal, beginning with Elena's recurring nightmare, the terrifying hallucinations, the failed cleansing, and the malevolent force that seemed to grow stronger with each passing day. She grew cold when she told him about finding Elena standing over Carrie and the chilling way she reacted.

"I also have something you must see," Maria said. She pulled out her phone and showed Tomas the pictures of the Latin words scratched into the table. "This happened yesterday, during *La Limpia*. Rocio said you might recognize the words."

Tomas's reaction was subtle but telling. His eyes darkened, and a shadow seemed to pass over his face. He stood abruptly, his chair scraping against the worn linoleum floor. For a moment, he seemed to struggle with an internal battle, his gaze fixed on the haunting images on her phone screen.

"I'm sorry, Maria. I can't help you," he said, his voice strained, the warmth replaced by a cold finality.

Maria was taken aback, and her heart sank. "But you haven't even heard everything. If you could just—"

Tomas cut her off, his demeanor resolute. "I have

much to do here. I am truly sorry for what you and your friend are going through." His eyes, once filled with compassion, now guarded and distant, told her that this door was closed.

"So you're really not going to help?" Maria's voice cracked, disbelief and despair mingling in her plea.

"I cannot." Tomas's reply was somber. "Please, I have much to do."

Maria's heart pounded in her chest as she processed Tomas's words, refusing to accept his dismissal so easily. The desperation and fear for Elena's safety fueled her persistence.

"But you must understand, Tomas, Elena's life is at stake. You've seen what an evil entity can do," Maria implored, her voice laced with desperation. "You have the knowledge, the experience. Who else can we turn to if not you?"

Tomas paced the small office, his steps echoing the turmoil within. "Maria, I understand more than you know," he said, stopping to face her, his expression pained. "But my past... I cannot risk another life. The church has banished me, and with good reason. What happened was a tragedy I cannot repeat."

Maria stepped closer, her resolve strengthening. "But isn't it a greater risk to do nothing? To let this evil continue to harm Elena and possibly others? Father, you have a chance to make things right, to use your gifts for good."

Tomas shook his head, the weight of his decision visible in the lines etched deeply on his face. "It's not about making things right for me. It's about preventing more harm. What happened...it haunts me every day. I was arrogant, thinking I could control forces of such pure evil. I won't make that mistake again."

"Then guide me," Maria pressed, her voice firm with determination. "If you cannot directly involve yourself, tell me what to do, point me in the right direction. Anything."

For a moment, it seemed as though Tomas might relent, his eyes searching hers, wrestling with an internal debate. But then he sighed, a sound heavy with resignation. "Maria, I'm sorry. Truly, I am. But involving myself, even as a guide...it could bring worse consequences. The church is still watching me, and what is happening to your friend...it's beyond what you understand."

Maria felt a surge of frustration, her hands clenching into fists at her sides. "So what? We just wait for Elena to be completely overtaken? For her to...to lose herself entirely?"

"I wish there was another way," Tomas said, his voice barely above a whisper. "I will pray for Elena, for you. But my hands are tied."

The finality in his tone left Maria feeling as if a cold hand had squeezed her heart. She stared at Tomas, searching for any sign of hope but finding none. The man before her was a fortress sealed by regret and caution.

With a heavy heart, she nodded, the fight draining out of her. "I'm sorry I wasted my time," Maria said, her voice bitter, filled with anger.

As Maria walked back to her car, the weight of Tomas's refusal settled over her like a shroud. The drive back to the apartment was a blur, her mind racing with fear for Elena and the dark road that lay ahead. She knew one thing with certainty: giving up was not an option. She would find another way to save her friend, no matter the cost.

Sixteen

Back at the apartment, Maria was surprised yet elated to see Elena sitting at the kitchen island. She looked refreshed, as though nearly twenty-four hours of sleep had miraculously rejuvenated her. Unable to contain her joy, Maria ran to Elena and embraced her tightly.

"I am so happy to see you up and around," Maria said. Over Elena's shoulder, she looked at Carrie and raised her eyebrows.

Carrie mouthed, "Tell you later."

"I'm happy to see you, too," Elena whispered.

"So what's going on here, ladies?" Maria asked. By the looks on their faces, it was clear she'd interrupted a serious conversation.

"There's something you should see in the closet," Carrie said, pushing up from the stool.

Maria followed the two women into Elena's room. The closet door stood open, and Maria stopped at the threshold, each hand gripping the frame on either side of the door. Her eyes were immediately drawn to the black fungus that had drastically expanded overnight to approximately the size of a manhole cover. The fuzzy, inky tendrils of the vile stuff spread across the ceiling, like splayed fingers of a malignant hand.

After a moment of stunned silence, Maria crossed the room, commandeering the dressing table chair and dragging it into the closet. She stepped up onto the chair, and immediately, Carrie and Elena reacted like worried parents. Carrie shouted, "Don't do that," while Elena said, "Be careful!" showing their concern for Maria's safety.

Ignoring them, Maria smirked and closely examined the demon goo. Up close, the substance appeared porous yet brittle. She prodded one of the tendrils gently with her forefinger—Carrie and Elena both gasped and in unison yelled, "Don't do that!"—and then pulled away quickly. She'd expected it to be warm, but it was cold to the touch.

She examined her finger, noting that some of the

demon goo remained on the tip. It felt tingly, as though it possessed some sort of numbing qualities. She sniffed it—drawing another duo of gasps—and said, "It smells like rotten eggs. And now I need to get this off my finger cause it's nasty!"

She jumped down and ran for the bathroom, turned the faucet full blast, and pumped Soft Soap into her cupped hands and worked her hands back and forth fervently. She lathered and scrubbed her finger under hot water until she couldn't stand the heat any longer.

Turning to dry her hands, Elena and Carrie crowded the bathroom. "Let me see," Carrie said, grabbing Maria's hand and scowling.

"Did it burn?" Elena queried. "Are you okay?"

Pulling her hand away, Maria said, "I'm fine. Chill, ladies."

Gently pushing past them, Maria walked back toward the closet, extracting her phone from her back pocket.

Carrie asked, "What are you doing now?"

"I'm going to snap some pics so we can track the spread," Maria said and looked back over her shoulder. "And so we can show this to someone."

Elena and Carrie glanced at each other. Elena said, "I didn't even think of that."

Maria snapped several pictures from various angles of the closet. She used the zoom function on the phone to get closeups so that she wouldn't give Elena and Carrie heart palpitations by climbing back onto the chair.

Outside the closet, the three gathered to look at the photos. Maria scrolled through them, pausing briefly on each and pinching the screen to zoom in and out so they could see the details clearly. On the fourth image, a buzzer sounded, and they all startled.

They froze and stared at each other, each woman's panic clearly plastered across their faces. Elena broke her paralysis and hissed, "Shit, that's the takeout we ordered."

"Holy shit," Carrie said and let out her breath in a rush. "I think I might have pissed myself."

Looking down at Carrie, Maria said, "Nope, you're good," and the three of them laughed nervously.

In the kitchen, Elena buzzed the Door Dasher in, waiting for him to leave the food behind the door and descend to the second floor before she opened the door and retrieved their food. While she unpacked the aromatic containers from the plastic bags, Carrie and Maria retrieved dishes and cups from the cupboard. Elena plated food and poured them each a cup of diet soda from the two-liter bottle.

They were all starving and dove in. Carrie and Maria hadn't eaten since the deep-dish pizza last night—Maria had actually been looking forward to eating the leftovers—and Elena couldn't remember when she'd last eaten, which frightened her a bit.

"This is so good," Maria said. "What is it?"

"Pad see eiw," Elena said.

"Are those real words?"

Carrie laughed and coughed as the food went down the wrong pipe.

"That's what the dish is called," Elena said. "You've never had Thai food?"

Maria shook her head and shoved a fork full of flat rice noodles into her mouth. She mumbled, "No, but it's fantastic."

After clearing her throat and drinking half her glass of diet soda, Carrie said, "Tell us what you've been up to today."

"What have you gotten yourself into?" Elena asked, dipping a prawn roll into the delicious, sweet sauce.

Maria finished chewing her noodles and set

down her fork. "I went back to see Rocio to try to convince her to help."

"What? I thought you went to school," Elena said.

"Today is Saturday."

"Right," Elena said. "Well, you didn't have to do that. Probably shouldn't have."

"I know I didn't have to. And I definitely should have."

"Don't keep us in suspense," Carrie said. "Did you convince her or not?"

"Not." Maria put her fork down now that the conversation took a more serious turn. "It's not that she doesn't want to help, it's that...she's outmatched. She's scared out of her mind after what happened yesterday."

"I can only imagine," Carrie said sympathetically.

"But she gave me the name of a man she thinks may be able to help," Maria continued. She picked up her phone, opened the photos app again, and scrolled past the demon goo images until she found what she was looking for. She held up the phone so the two teachers could see it. "It's the Latin words that were scratched into the table."

Carrie took the phone from Maria and used her

thumb and forefinger to spread the image on the screen for a closer look. She hadn't been with Elena and Maria during the horrifying cleansing debacle, and she was seeing this for the first time. To Maria, she asked, "Do you know what it says?"

"No," Maria said. "Rocio didn't, either, but she says Tomas will know and whatever it says might convince him to help."

"Who is Tomas?" Elena asked.

Taking the phone back from Carrie, Maria said, "According to Rocio, he was a priest."

"Was?" Carrie asked.

"She said he was *excommunicated*. I had to look it up. Basically, he did something really bad and now he's doing penance at a food pantry until he can get back into the good graces of the church."

Elena asked, "What exactly does a priest have to do to be excommunicated?"

"He performed an exorcism without permission," Maria said, purposefully leaving out the fact that a young boy died during the ritual.

"A rebel priest sounds exactly like what we need. Let's talk to him," Carrie said.

"I already did," Maria said. She picked up her fork and speared a piece of tender beef. She looked up at Carrie. "He wasn't interested."

"Wasn't interested?" Elena asked.

"What does that mean?" Carried blurted. "Not interested?"

"He doesn't do...exorcism stuff anymore since the church banned him. But when I showed him the Latin words...he definitely recognized them, though he tried to play it off like he didn't."

"You sure he recognized the words?" Carrie asked.

"I'm positive. And as soon as he saw them, his demeanor changed. He got cold, and he asked me to leave."

The women both looked dejected, and Maria felt horrible for deflating their spirits at the dinner table. Elena was quiet, no doubt feeling hopeless.

Maria said, "But I'm sure we can convince him to help. He just needs...the right motivation."

"How do we motivate a priest?" Elena asked.

"Donations," Carrie mumbled.

Maria laughed. "That could work, maybe. The food pantry could certainly use an infusion of cash. But I was thinking we show him the pictures of the demon goo and ask him to translate the Latin. Force him to become involved."

"And that's going to work?" Carrie asked.

"I don't know. Probably not. But this time, he's

going to have to deal with all three of us. And Elena is going to convince him to help."

"I am?"

"Yeah, you are," Carrie said and put an arm around Elena. "But that's for tomorrow. Tonight is girl's night!"

SEVENTEEN

TOMAS LOCKED UP THE FOOD PANTRY AS DUSK PAINTED the sky in shades of deep purples and oranges. He climbed the narrow staircase leading to the apartment above the storefront, a space that could generously be described as "cozy" but flirted with the boundaries of legality in terms of living conditions. Yet, after spending years in makeshift shelters across Africa and Venezuela during his years with the church, Tomas found a sort of grim comfort here. The place was clean and had running water and an air conditioner that wheezed more than it cooled, but more importantly, it was affordable.

Inside, he tossed the keys onto a side table and placed his wallet and phone beside them. Crossing the room in the dark with the ease of a man well acquainted with his surroundings, he switched on a small lamp that sat atop an end table. He shrugged out of his tweed jacket and draped it casually over the back of the sofa.

In the cramped bedroom, he undressed, hanging his pants and shirt on wire hangers on a hook behind the door so they wouldn't get wrinkled. The lack of a closet was made up for with stackable plastic drawers from Walmart where he kept the remainder of his meager wardrobe, mostly second-hand clothing from donations. In the cramped bathroom, he started the shower, then sat on the toilet to do his business while he waited for the water to warm up.

After relieving himself, he turned off the overhead light so that the room was dark and stepped into the shower stall, pulling the curtain closed. Leaning against the plastic wall liners, he closed his eyes, the hot water acting as a balm, seeping deep into muscles. The steam was a shroud, a momentary retreat from the outside world.

He remained in the shower until the hot water ran cold, which wasn't nearly long enough. Drying off, he noted the growing length of his hair and beard and his overall disheveled look. He needed a cut and trim, yet he could not justify the cost. He'd wait until his hair grew out longer, probably another couple of weeks, before seeking out a community barber. In the meantime, he wiped fog off the medicine cabinet mirror and used a pair of scissors to trim some fly-aways from his beard.

In the bedroom, Tomas pulled on a pair of boxer shorts that were worn in the seat—and a size too large for his frame—and a sleeveless T-shirt. In the kitchenette, he microwaved two Hot Pockets (barbecue chicken flavor, not his favorite, but he couldn't be picky when he had more than most). The hum of the microwave was a familiar background noise in the quiet of his kitchen, where he leaned against the sink, waiting for his dinner.

When his food was warmed, he retrieved a bottle of spring water from a half-empty case on the floor by the refrigerator. The luxury of bottled water, provided by a generous donation from a local supplier who dropped off several pallets for the pantry, each stacked with forty-eight cases, was a treat compared to the chemical taste of Chicago tap water.

He sat on the battered secondhand sofa, set his food on the scarred television tray that looked like an antique circa the 1960s, then turned on the news. He ate slowly while news anchors droned on about the horrible tragedies of the world until their words became unrecognizable speech emanating from talking heads.

Later, as he sat on the worn sofa with the empty paper plate on the TV tray, his mind wandered back to the encounter this morning with the young woman, Maria. Her desperation, her fear for her friend, stirred within Tomas horrible memories and profound guilt of his tragic past.

Tomas had once walked with unwavering faith until the nightmarish exorcism tore his world apart. The victim, a boy of merely twelve, had been ensnared by a demon so vile, the mere memory of it sent shivers skittering down Tomas's spine even now. The ordeal that unfolded was grueling, a test of endurance for both the possessed and the exorcist. Ironically, it wasn't the demon's malevolence that claimed the young life; it was the exorcism itself— his heart, overwhelmed by fear and exhaustion, simply gave out.

The shadow of the boy's death clung to Tomas like an unshakable pall, a daily reminder of his miscalculation, his arrogance, and the disillusionment of the church in him.

Sleep, when it came to Tomas, was a cruel mistress, blurring the lines between the day's weariness and the haunting specters of his past. He drifted into a dream, more a memory, finding himself back in that suffocating room in the Venezuelan jungle where the battle for the boy's soul had played out. The air was thick, laced with the scent of incense and the unmistakable odor of raw fear. The prayers he invoked echoed back at him, empty and mocking, as if the room itself scorned his efforts.

The boy, a figure of pure torment, with eyes that reflected an abyssal darkness, spoke in a cacophony of voices that seemed to claw their way out of the depths of hell. The palpable presence of the demon pressed down on Tomas, as real as the sweat that beaded on his forehead, its wickedness coiling around his heart with a vice-like grip. In a moment of demonic frenzy, the boy's shirt was torn away, flung against the wall as if discarded by an unseen force. Etched into the vulnerable flesh of his abdomen, as though by the claws of the beast itself, were the words: "*Haec anima mea est.*"

The boy's screams reverberated through the thin walls, rumbling through the floor beneath Tomas's feet. In desperation, Tomas wanted to clamp hands over his ears, his eyes squeezed shut, as he whispered the Lord's Prayer, a plea for divine intervention. The crucifix he desperately clutched drew blood from his palm, as if the sacred object itself resisted his touch.

"*Stop!*"

The command tore from Tomas's throat, born of both desperation and dwindling hope. Abruptly, silence descended, a heavy, oppressive silence. Cautiously, Tomas opened his eyes. The boy's gaze met his, no longer veiled in darkness but brimming with terror and agony. With a feeble effort, the boy reached out, his voice a whisper, "*Ayúdame, padre,*" ("Help me, Father") before his body succumbed, collapsing into a grotesque tableau of death.

Tomas's breath hitched, frozen in a moment of sheer, palpable dread. He edged closer to the bedside, the silence of the room amplifying the erratic pounding of his heart. His hands shook as his fingertips brushed against the icy skin to check for the faintest hint of life, the stillness shattered without warning.

In a swift, horrifying jolt, the boy's hand shot up, latching onto Tomas's wrist with a grip as cold and unyielding as iron. Tomas's heart leaped into his throat, a scream choked off before it could escape. The boy's eyes snapped open, revealing a pair of deep, blood-red orbs that burned with an unholy light. A voice, as if dredged from the depths of hell itself, rumbled through the room, *"This soul is mine!"* The declaration thundered in Tomas's ears, a promise of darkness so profound it seemed to suck the very light from the room, leaving a suffocating cloak of shadow that threatened to swallow him whole.

Tomas awoke with a start, his breath ragged, the echoes of the boy's plea still ringing in his ears. The dream, a recurring visitor in the solitude of the night, left him shaken.

The dream wasn't just a memory; it felt like a warning, a premonition perhaps, linking the tragedy of the past with the present, like pieces of a puzzle that seemed to point toward a familiar malevolent force.

As the night stretched on, Tomas sat in the darkness, the only light coming from the streetlamp outside casting long shadows across the room. He pondered the connection between the inscriptions Maria showed him and the demon he had once failed to banish. The haunting dream and the eerie parallels to his past, woven into the tapestry of his own haunted memories, suggested a connection that was more than coincidental and impossible to ignore.

EIGHTEEN

THE FOLLOWING MORNING, TOMAS WAS NOT SURPRISED when the three women showed up at the pantry shortly after opening. The young woman, Maria, had been adamant that he help her friend. She did not appear to him to be the type to easily give up on anything once she'd set her mind to it, and he was right about that.

He turned over his clipboard—he'd been in the middle of inventorying canned goods in the main room, policing expiration dates and damaged products—to one of his volunteers and then waved at them to catch their attention and signaled for them to follow him. Without a word, he led them to the cramped office just off the kitchen where a volunteer staff made soups, sandwiches, and other low-cost meals that could feed the masses during lunch service. Around noon, they'd open their doors to the unhoused and less fortunate in the Pilsen community.

The office was dark, even after Tomas switched on the overhead light, which gave off a sickly yellow hue. A small wood desk, patinated by age, sat at the center of the small room. Two six-foot metal bookcases, donated by the local library upon its closing, stood sentinel behind the desk, housing Tomas's extensive collection of books from his seminary days, as well as a plethora of other books of Catholic faith.

After asking them to sit in the guest chairs opposite his desk, which was a tight fit, given the dimension of the room—Carrie and Elena sat in the two available seats, while Maria stood behind them—Tomas slowly lowered himself into his own chair behind the scarred desk.

Directing his attention to Maria, Tomas said, "I see you've brought reinforcements this morning."

"This is Carrie and Elena," Maria said, ignoring his subtle passive-aggressive remark, her hand unconsciously hovering above each woman's head as she introduced them. "I wanted you to meet Elena and to hear her experiences directly."

"To see if she can convince me when you could not?" Tomas smiled.

"Yes," Maria admitted openly. "And we also have something to show you that we hope convinces you how seriously we need your help."

Maria pulled out her phone and opened the photos app, then, reaching between Carrie and Elena, placed the phone on the desk and slid it toward Tomas. He looked at the phone for a moment, as if considering whether or not he would even entertain them.

"Please," Elena said, "just take a look. That's all we ask. And for you to hear us out."

After a tense moment, Tomas plucked a pair of reading glasses from the front pocket of his plaid shirt and slipped them on before finally picking up the phone.

"There was a time I did not need these," Tomas said, indicating the plastic frame readers. "But I must embrace the inevitable."

With his readers on, he examined the image, turning the phone in his hand, then using his fingers to enlarge the image for a closer look. He scrolled through the three or four images Maria had snapped, and they could tell by his expression he was genuinely intrigued.

"Where is this photo from?" he asked, unconsciously stroking the ends of his beard with his free hand.

"Elena's closet," Maria answered.

Tomas slid his reading glasses off the bridge of his nose and held one temple pinched between his thumb and forefinger, resting his hand on the desk. He lowered Maria's phone and looked at the three women sitting across from him, awash in the pale light of the yellowed bulb in the dusty fixture above.

"Do you know what that is, Father?" Carrie asked, more so to break the awkward silence.

"I'm no longer a priest. I suppose I'm on indefinite leave. Just call me Tomas," he responded. His gaze lingered on the image of the black fungus, his expression one of solemn contemplation. Finally, he looked at Elena and asked, "When did this appear?"

Elena's eyes shifted toward the ceiling as she considered the question. Time was difficult for her lately, as the days seemed to blur together, or she'd lost time. "About a week ago, I think." She looked at Carrie—who nodded—for confirmation. "It appeared the morning after I first lost time."

"After you lost time? Tell me about that," Tomas said, now more keenly interested.

"I remember trying to watch television after dinner to take my mind off what happened earlier in the day. I couldn't stop thinking about the hallucinations—did Maria tell you about them?"

Tomas nodded.

"Good, because I don't think I can talk about that again, at least not right now. I just couldn't stop thinking about it then, wondering if what I saw was real or if I was losing my mind. I just couldn't understand what was happening to me, why it was happening. And I'd just got suspended from my job, so I was just so stressed. Anyway, I was watching television, and the phone rang. It was Carrie. She'd been calling all afternoon—we'd had an argument at work, but that's neither here nor there—but I was upset with her, didn't want to talk to her. I picked up the phone and shut off the ringer. The next thing I remember, I was standing outside my bedroom closet with a ladder and flashlight. I have no recollection of the time in between the phone call or retrieving the ladder and flashlight. When I noted the time, the nearly eight hours that had passed between that are...completely blank."

"Should I tell him about the phone call?" Carrie asked, looking at Elena, who nodded.

"The call from you she didn't take?" Tomas asked.

"Yes and no," Carrie said. "Elena didn't take the call...but I certainly had a conversation with her. I don't know if I was actually talking to her and she doesn't remember or...or I don't know what. But she answered, and she said some very mean things that were definitely *not* characteristic of Elena," Carrie said, looking again at Elena and touching her arm. "Then there was a sharp piercing sound. I dropped the phone, then picked it up, and there were voices, like hundreds of voices, all at once, speaking a language I didn't understand, repeating the same thing over and over and over again, the voices getting louder until the phone disconnected."

"And you don't remember talking to Carrie that night?" Tomas asked.

"No, not at all. But I suppose, thinking back on it, it's possible but I just don't remember."

"Hmm," Tomas muttered abstractly as he digested the information.

"Elena had a...physical experience that night," Maria said, after Tomas's long pause. "With *la vieja malvada*."

Tomas looked at Elena with raised eyebrows in anticipation of an explanation.

"The old woman that appeared in my recurring nightmares. I don't know who or what she is... I just know that she's a vile, evil thing."

"That night, *la vieja* attacked her in the attic," Maria said. She considered telling Tomas about her dream, or rather how she was somehow a participant and how the old woman scratched her, but she didn't want him to shift his focus from Elena again.

"A couple days earlier, when I woke from the nightmare, I thought I saw something in the closet. I thought it was my imagination, that the fear of the nightmare was clinging to me upon waking, but I couldn't go back to sleep without confirming it wasn't...something *real*. I searched the entire apartment, every room, and found nothing. The only place I hadn't checked was the attic space above the closet. I was too frightened to open the hatch and check that night."

"Quite understandable," Tomas said.

"But that night after the call, when I found myself in the closet with the ladder and flashlight, I felt compelled to open the hatch and have a look up there. I felt...obsessed, you know? Like I *had* to know for sure if something was up there." Elena took a deep breath before telling Tomas about the old woman's attack, the tongue with snake heads entering her mouth. She shuddered as she spoke, felt chilled. "I woke the next morning on the floor of the closet. The attic hatch was sealed, and the spot was there," Elena finished.

Tomas listened again, his face a blank slate. Pointing to the phone where the image of the fungus remained on screen, he asked, "And this was the size of a quarter then?"

Elena nodded.

"Can you show me those first photos of the substance?"

Elena frowned. "We don't have them. We didn't think about...*documenting* the phenomenon, at least not until last night. It was Maria's idea."

"I thought it would be important to track the rate of spread," Maria said.

Tomas nodded. "That's good. Continue to do that."

"So what is it?" Carrie asked, referring to what Maria called the demon goo. "It obviously has something to do with...whatever's happening to Elena. Is it a sign of...oh, I hate to say the word, but a sign of demonic activity?"

Tomas sighed. "In my time with the church, I've

encountered many things that defy simple explanation. Sometimes, natural phenomena can be influenced by spiritual disturbances. It's not for me to say if it's a sign of demonic presence without more evidence."

"Can you look at the next photo, please?" Maria asked.

Tomas slid the glasses back on and swiped to the next photo, the image of the words, in Latin, scratched onto the surface of Rocio's table. He looked at it for nearly thirty seconds before slowly taking off the glasses again, this time setting them down. He slid the phone back toward Maria, though she left it laying on the desk.

"You showed me this yesterday."

Maria nodded. "It's familiar to you, isn't it? I saw in your face that you recognized the words."

When Tomas did not answer, Carrie asked, "What does it say? You can read it, can't you?"

Clasping his hands in front of him, Tomas said, "It roughly translates to, 'This soul is mine.'"

A palpable silence fell over the room. A cold shiver snaked down Elena's spine, and her heart thudded against her chest as if seeking escape from the dire prophecy those words promised. Maria and

Carrie exchanged a glance, a mix of fear and deep concern etched across their features.

Carrie reached out, her hand trembling, and clasped Elena's in an unspoken vow of support. Maria's jaw set hard against the rising tide of panic that seemed to explode in her stomach, like a sudden blast of indigestion. She looked at Tomas, her eyes burning with a resolve.

"Where have you seen that message before?" she asked, her voice steady but her fear unmistakable.

"That doesn't matter," Tomas said in a firm tone of finality. He focused his attention on Elena with more intensity than previously. With a new grit to his voice, he asked, "Have you or anyone close to you been involved with the occult, witchcraft, or any rituals that are not in line with the Church's teachings?"

Elena looked shocked. "No, of course not!"

"Do you hear voices that no one else can or feel unseen presences around you?"

Elena swallowed. "Yes, you know that."

"Have you experienced any unexplainable physical afflictions or markings on your body?" Tomas asked.

"Yes."

"Show him," Maria prompted.

Hesitantly, Elena stood and slowly lifted her shirt, revealing the bruises along her flank. "I woke one morning and found these. I don't know how it happened, and it was a separate incident from the attic."

Tomas leaned forward and briefly examined her in the pale light of the room. After a moment, he said, "Thank you. Please lower your shirt."

He waited for Elena to do as instructed. When she was seated again, he said, "Elena, do certain sacred objects or places cause you distress or physical reactions?"

"No," she said, "At least...I don't think so."

"I'd like to give you something," Tomas said.

He slid back slightly in his chair so that he could access the middle drawer of the desk. Shifting the items within, he located what he was looking for after a few seconds, then closed the drawer. He placed the object he'd retrieved from the drawer onto the desk and rested his forefinger over it. The object was small and flat, the size of a coin.

With his eyes focused on Elena, Tomas slid the object across the surface directly in front of her. His eyes never leaving her, he lifted his finger, revealing a medallion. The silver was slightly faded and worn, as though the medal had been handled often. On the face of it was the figure of Saint Joseph, a compassionate and strong figure, holding the infant Jesus in one arm and a carpenter's square in his other hand.

"This is Saint Joseph," Tomas said evenly. "He is oftentimes referred to as the terror of demons given his role as protector of the Holy Family. He embodies piety and righteousness, making him a formable enemy against evil. Elena, I want you to have this. Please pick it up."

Elena stared at the medallion, at first with a mixture of curiosity and apprehension. A few seconds ticked by before she tentatively reached out for the offered object. However, her hand trembled and stopped about six inches from the holy trinket. Though she tried, she suddenly could not move her hand closer to the token. It was as if an invisible force physically restrained her movement.

Maria placed a hand on Elena's shoulder and said, "Elena, pick it up."

"I will," she said through gritted teeth.

Her fingers hovered inches from the medallion, and she strained the muscles of her arm and shoulder, attempting to push through an invisible boundary between her and the representation of Saint Joseph.

Carrie shifted in her chair, the first flicker of fear gnawing at her belly. She seemed to notice a palpable shift in the aura of the room, especially around Elena. "Elena? Why won't you pick it up?"

"Pick up the medallion," Tomas said firmly. "Accept Saint Joseph into your life. Accept him as your protector."

Elena's reaction to his words was immediate and guttural, her eyes widening in terror. "I can't," she gasped, pulling her hand away. "I can't!"

"Pick it up!" Tomas demanded and slammed his fist against the desk, rattling the objects upon it.

"Okay, that's enough," Carrie interjected, startled, her voice tinged with immediate concern.

Maria grasped Carrie's shoulders. "Let him work," she whispered, her voice low but firm. She realized this was a test, that Tomas was attempting to evoke a response from the entity. He was addressing it directly, not Elena.

Carrie, though clearly conflicted, fell silent, biting her lip and nodding reluctantly. Her gaze lingered on Elena, watching her expressions and demeanor and not recognizing her friend.

"Pick it up, Elena," Maria encouraged her again.

Elena's reaction was visceral. Her posture stiffened, and a sheen of sweat broke out across her forehead though the room was not warm or stifling. Her breathing became labored, and her eyes darted around the room as if she were a caged animal seeking an escape.

"I don't... I feel sick," she stammered, her voice laced with acute dread.

Ignoring her obvious discomfort, not addressing Elena, but rather the evil within, Tomas asked, "When you manipulate her actions, causing harm and despair, how do you justify this theft of life?"

Elena made an involuntary mewling sound. "Please, stop," she whispered, clutching her stomach, her face suddenly contorted in distress.

Standing suddenly, Tomas picked up the medallion of Saint Joseph. With determination, he stepped around the desk, closing the distance between them.

Elena immediately tried to back away, but Tomas was quick. He pressed the medallion to the back of Elena's hand. Suddenly, a spasm of revulsion contorted her features. Her hand snapped back as if burned, and a low growl, alien and menacing, escaped her lips—a sound too guttural, too primal to belong to her. Her body language became defensive, a clear indication of the demon's aversion to the holy artifact.

Elena's chair scraped aggressively against the

floor as she violently pushed back from the desk, pinning Maria between the chair and the wall. She sprang from the chair and shouldered her way through Carrie without any regard for her friend, almost knocking her to the floor before bolting from the oppressive chamber.

After a moment of stunned silence, Carrie hurried after Elena. Alone in the room with Tomas, Maria yelled, "What more proof do you need? Will you help her now?"

Tomas, acknowledging the critical stage of Elena's possession, nodded. "I will come tonight. We must make haste. I must prepare."

Elena raced through the maze of aisles, clawing her way through until she reached the front door. She realized she must have looked like a madwoman running through the pantry, doubled over, clutching at her abdomen like a woman about to give birth to something inhuman. She staggered several steps away from the entrance, almost losing her balance before she bent forward, one hand pressed against her abdomen while she steadied herself against the brick wall of the building with the other.

An inexplicable sense of dread flooded her senses. A sudden chill seeped into her bones like an icy grip clutching her heart with fingers as cold as death itself. Despite the brevity of the contact with the Saint Joseph medallion, the sensation was agonizingly intense, the very purity of the blessed object burned through to the entity inside. The demon within had recoiled, its dark essence writhing in torment as the sanctity of the object clashed with its corruption.

Her stomach churned, and she heaved, spewing milky, mucous-like vomit onto the pavement. She gagged, tried to catch her breath, but then vomited again, the foul-smelling substance exiting not only her mouth but also expelled from her nostrils. Her breathing was ragged and rapid as she focused on controlling her gorge, attempting to catch her breath and keep from retching again. Her skin crawled as if swarmed by unseen insects, muscles twitched uncontrollably, and pain seared through her veins like molten lead.

A profound sense of violation stirred deep within Elena; a guttural terror erupted in her belly like corrosive acid, burning the lining of her stomach. The sacred token pressed against her skin had laid bare the blasphemy inside her, ripping open a festering wound that whispered dark prophecies of her damnation. It heralded the onset of an eternal struggle, a battle waged between the sacred and the profane over the destiny of her soul.

NINETEEN

ELENA FELT AN OVERWHELMING COMPULSION TO isolate herself, driven by the entity's desire to weaken her mental resistance, cutting her off from access to external support in an attempt to imprison her within her own mind where its control could dominate and become absolute.

As soon as she entered the condo, she ran directly to her bedroom. To isolate herself was an urgent, desperate, animalistic need, propelled by a sickness that seemed to gnaw at her very essence. Her symptoms were an infernal chorus of physical agony: a roiling stomach, a skull-splitting headache, and joints that burned as if engulfed in unseen flames. Yet this physical torment was but a shadow to the darker tumult stirring within her psyche, a tempest not entirely her own and one she could not control.

Upon reaching her bedroom, Elena whirled around on the two women, her posture defensive, as if the doorway were the last bastion against an encroaching darkness she was determined to shut out. Her voice was laced with a fury that felt both foreign and intimate.

"*Back the fuck off!*" she bellowed at Carrie and Maria, who followed closely behind like two fucking mother hens, giving her no room to breathe. "Can't I have a moment's privacy without you both up my ass?"

The words, though aimed at her friends, echoed the inner conflict wrought by the entity's influence. Her irritability toward Carrie's and Maria's ministrations the entire ride home from the food pantry had slowly morphed into an uncharacteristic rage, a stark contrast to her usual demeanor.

Despite understanding their intentions were pure, a venomous annoyance bubbled inside Elena, urging her to lash out, to seek isolation like an animal wanting to die alone. The vile internal force was amplifying her distress, twisting her thoughts and feelings into something alien.

After slamming the door on the two nagging

bitches, Elena barricaded herself within the confines of her bathroom, further away from their prying eyes and ears and their disingenuous concern for her well-being. The air within the room was ripe with the stench of desecration, a blend of sulfur and burned flesh, a pungent aroma that assaulted her senses. She felt vile, despicable, as if her very skin were tainted by the entity's foul essence.

A desperate need to rid herself of the vile stench drove her to strip out of her clothing. She tore the T-shirt over her head, struggled briefly with the button on her jeans, then skinned them off before pulling off her panties. She gathered up the clothing and threw them harshly into the trash bin.

Elena clawed at the shower knobs with stiff fingers until the water rushed from the faucet into the tub. She hastily pulled the diverter, activating the shower, and within moments, scalding-hot water began steaming the bathroom.

She leaned against the sink, bracing herself by placing her hands against the moist, marble counter. Leaning forward, she breathed deeply of the damp air as beads of sweat broke out across her forehead. Horrible spasming cramps pressed her belly outward, as if something inside was trying to tear its way out of her.

Her mind was ensnared by the harrowing memory of the priest's office as she recalled the searing pain of the holy medallion upon her flesh and the terrifying realization of the entity recoiling within her, a sinister usurper seizing control. That single act had awakened the evil within.

Amidst the rising steam that seemed to weigh down each breath she inhaled, the lights suddenly flickered, briefly creating a strobe-like effect. Through the misted mirror, rapid movement from left to right caught her attention, as if the mirror was a window and a shadow had run past.

Elena stood straight, breath caught in her throat, her eyes focused intensely on the fogged glass. A shadow passed again behind the silver veil of the steamed mirror. With one trembling hand, Elena slowly placed it against the mirror, pressing her hand on it until her palm was flat against the surface. With one quick swipe of her hand, she wiped away the film of fog.

A pair of glowing silver eyes peered back at her from behind the glass. A burst of adrenaline coursed through her veins, triggering her fight-or-flight response. She attempted to turn away from the evil eyes, to flee from their horrible, hypnotic gaze, but her feet were rooted and every muscle in her body stiffened. It was as if the malevolent orbs held her fixed against her will.

She felt herself drawn toward the mirror, her face slowly inching forward by pressure applied to back of her head by an unseen force. She grunted, strained against it, yet her face inched forward. When she was several inches away from the glowing eyes, *la vieja malvada's* face materialized from the shadows, its visage a tapestry of horror: skin mottled and gray, cracks like fissures spreading across in all directions, hair tangled and clumped in filthy knots, white-hot silver orbs gleaming with pure evil, and a mouth filled with razor-sharp teeth that seemed to split its lips when it grinned.

"*Anima tua mea est.*" ("Your soul is mine.")

Its gnarled, hooked hands shot through the mirror, gripping Elena's shoulders, the spade-like claws digging deep into her flesh like eagle's talons, scraping the skin off her clavicle. Elena tried to scream, her mouth stretched wide and her head thrown back, but no sound escaped her.

La vieja malvada violently shoved Elena across the room with supernatural force, her body crashing against the wall with a brutal impact. Her head thudded against the tile wall, and her body made a greasy sucking sound as she slid into the tub, her body limp. She tasted blood in her mouth, having bit her tongue.

Daze, on the verge of unconsciousness, Elena struggled to keep her eyes open. Hot water burned Elena's skin, and pain shot around from the back of her head, stabbing at the backs of her eyeballs. As she lay helpless in the tub, the hag loomed over her. One of its deflated breasts hung down through the torn flap of the filthy, tattered hospital gown. Yellow pus leaked from its nipple, like rotted condensed milk.

The hag worked its grotesque mouth. "*Dico animam tuam.*" ("I lay claim to your soul.")

One foot slapped against the tub as *la vieja malvada* came forward, slowly lifting its other leg over the lip before straddling Elena, pinning her arms against her own body. The demonic entity gripped Elena's throat with one gnarled and knotted hand while the other forced her mouth open, its disgusting fingers probing, splayed her clenched teeth, forcing her tongue down against her lower teeth.

Elena gagged as the hag leaned in, its silver eyes lit up like halogen fog lamps spearing the darkness. Slivers of vile saliva hung from cracked and chewed lips. From the depths of its gaping maw, the tongue slithered forth, grotesque and mottled with sores that oozed pink liquid. Two eyeless snake heads at its end thrust forward into Elena's gaping mouth, sliding down her throat like course grit sandpaper. The hag's grip relaxed as Elena's body convulsed uncontrollably in the bathtub, spasms of dark power wracking her body while blood began its slow trail from her nostrils.

In that moment, the darkness seemed to pulse with a malevolent life of its own, ensnaring her in a void where despair reigned sovereign. Elena drifted in an abyssal sea of horror, a realm from which escape seemed an impossible dream, a captive of the evil that now claimed dominion over her. This was the moment of complete possession, the point of no return where Elena's battle was lost to the darkness.

"Did you hear that?" Maria cried out, startled.

They had been seated on the floor, huddled outside Elena's bedroom when the initial commotion erupted from within. The sound, reminiscent of a shower rod clattering to the floor accompanied by a distressing, fleshy thump, suggested Elena's body colliding with a hard surface, like she'd fallen in the tub.

Maria stood quickly, her blood rushing to her face and coloring her cheeks. A sudden heat flushed over her, an uncomfortable warmth spreading across her face and making her hair tingle. She gripped the knob, turning it hard and shoving the bedroom door open with more force than she intended. The door struck the doorstop and rebounded, hitting her elbow smartly as she rushed across the room toward the bathroom.

"Elena?" Carrie's voice cracked as she called out from beside Maria as the two of them huddled behind the locked door. Carrie rattled the knob sharply. "Elena, are you okay? Please, open the door!" There was urgency in her voice, bordering on desperation.

Maria, her patience frayed by fear and her body driven by adrenaline, pounded on the door with a desperation born out of her escalating terror. "Elena! Please, let us in! Talk to us!"

Elena's silence was even more frightening. They looked at each other, fear and desperation apparent on both of their faces. As though reading each other's minds, both women squared their shoulders, stepping back, almost in unison, before delivering two forceful kicks to the bathroom door. The door, resistant at first, eventually gave way under their relentless assault, swinging open when the wood frame around the latch lock finally gave way.

The room was thick with heated steam. The floor was slick with water spray from the showerhead. Elena lay motionless in the tub, her body half covered by the fallen shower curtain, the water around her tainted a horrifying shade of pink with her blood.

"Oh my God, Elena!"

Carrie's scream, a raw sound of terror, echoed off the walls. The sight of bruises marring Elena's neck and the trickle of blood from her nose and ear painted a picture of violence and chaos that chilled them both deep within their marrow.

Reacting with a mechanical efficiency born of shock, Carrie and Maria lifted Elena from the tub. They carried her to the bedroom, laying her gently on the bed, her form limp and appearing lifeless, her eyes open but unseeing, a silent witness to the nightmare only she could fathom.

"Elena, please," Carrie pleaded. She took Elena's face gently in both of her hands. "Say something. Please."

Maria, ever practical in the face of crisis, fetched

a damp cloth from the bathroom. Stepping in front of Carrie, she used the damp cloth to gently clean the blood from Elena's face.

Carrie found Elena's bathrobe hanging over the back of the dressing table chair and scooped it up. She waited for Maria to finish her task, and then with the younger girl's assistance, they struggled to dress Elena's naked body in the robe. Working together, they rolled her onto one side, gently guiding her arm through the sleeve and draping the robe across her back, then rolled her over and did the same. With Elena on her back, Carrie folded the ends of the robe across her and secured it with the robe tie.

They retreated to the foot of the bed and looked helpless at their comatose friend, both unsure what to do next. After a moment, Carrie took Maria's hand.

"We need to call her mother," Maria said after a few moments. She looked at Carrie, whose attention was still focused on Elena. Shaking Carrie's hand to get her attention, Maria repeated, "We need to call her mother."

"Her mother?" Carrie responded, confused. "We need to call an ambulance. She needs medical attention."

"We already talked about this. You know they can't help her. She's beyond fucking doctors and shrinks, Carrie," Maria countered, her words a harsh reminder of the grim reality they faced. "You know what will happen. I mean look, she can't even speak for herself. They'll just put her in a fucking padded room and forget about her."

The frustration and helplessness that had been simmering beneath the surface erupted in Carrie. Her voice rising, she yelled, "We are *not* equipped to handle this. What are we even doing here?"

"Get a grip," Maria said, her voice firm. Releasing Carrie's hand and grabbing her by the shoulders, she said, "We're here for Elena. Your best friend. Yes, this is all kinds of messed up and way beyond you or me, but we're all she has. You understand?"

Carrie swallowed hard, the gravity of their situation overwhelming her. Nodding, she found a semblance of resolve in Maria's words. "Yeah, yeah, I'm with you. I'm with you. Sorry."

"Don't apologize. You and me, we've got this. We've got each other, right?"

Maria's words fortified Carrie, a reminder that together, they could face the nightmare before them. "Yes, we've got each other. We've got Elena."

Maria handed Carrie the phone. Accepting it,

Carrie closed her eyes, taking a deep breath, seeking a moment of peace in the eye of this completely fucked-up shitstorm.

"I don't know Elena's mom. I've never met her or spoke to her. What do I even say? 'Hey, Ms. Vera, you don't know me, but I'm your daughter's friend, and I'm calling to tell you she's possessed by a demonic entity!'"

Maria was far more patient and focused than she had any right to be. Calmly, she took Elena's phone from Carrie's trembling hands, offered a small, reassuring smile. "It's okay, I've got this."

With the phone in hand, she went around the bed and stood beside Elena. The blank look on her face and the way her glazed eyes stared at the ceiling unnerved her. Leaning over her teacher, Maria brushed away the strands of wet hair from her face, a gesture of tenderness and caring. "I'm sorry, but I need to do this," she said, hoping that Elena could hear her and know they were with her. She held the phone in front of Elena's face, unlocking it with Face ID.

With access to the phone, Maria stood up and joined Carrie at the foot of the bed. She located "Mommy" in Elena's favorites contact list and pressed the call button. As the phone rang, she turned away and began pacing the room.

Carrie remained fixed at the foot of the bed, nervously chewing at her fingernails. Maria spoke to Elena's mother in Spanish, her voice a blend of urgency and reassurance. Carrie admired the girl, was completely awed by her strength and tenacity. She was intelligent, thinking of things Elena and Carrie hadn't even considered. And she was compassionate and loyal. In that moment, Carrie felt completely helpless and inadequate. She realized that if she'd had to face this alone, without Maria, she'd be lost and Elena's fate would be sealed.

"She's coming," Maria said after ending the call. She accessed the phone's setting and quickly disabled the Face ID feature and set a simple PIN, sharing it with Carrie, so that either of them could access the phone later if needed.

"Now what, kid?" Carrie asked. "Do we call Tomas?"

Maria shook her head, her gaze steady and her voice was calm. "No. He'll come soon. But for now, we just wait. And pray."

TWENTY

LUISA WHITE-KNUCKLED THE STEERING WHEEL THE entire hour-and-a-half drive from Rockford to Chicago. Speeding down I-90 at more than eighty miles an hour, she kept replaying the conversation with the young girl over and over in her mind. The girl hadn't told her much over the phone—she was careful choosing her words, but the urgency behind them was very clear—but Luisa knew that the ancient evil that had plagued her family for two generations had returned. Fleeing from Ecuador, putting over three thousand miles and the sea between them, was not enough to keep the evil from finding them, from finding Elena.

The evening sky was a dark canvas of dramatic hues that mirrored Luisa's emotional state. After a while of driving in silence, she switched on the satellite radio and tuned into a podcast from one of her favorite comedians in an attempt to keep her mind from going further into the dark places. Although deep down, she always feared this would happen, that the demon would return, the passage of years allowed for false hope. She understood now it had only been biding its time.

Nearly half an hour later, she exited the highway and navigated the streets until finally reaching her destination. She found street parking three blocks down from Elena's building, cursing the shitty parking in the neighborhood. The streetlamps cast long shadows across the sidewalk as she hurried along, gripping the collar of her sweater tightly against her throat as she walked against the crisp night breeze, her rapid footsteps echoing back from the facades of two- and three-story buildings that flanked both sides of the street.

At the front entrance to the building, Luisa impatiently pressed the bell for her daughter's apartment, her foot tapping nervously against the concrete step while she waited. The buzz finally sounded, and the outer door unlocked, allowing her access to the building. She rushed up the three flights of stairs blindly, too fast for a woman her age, but not caring if she fell or twisted an ankle.

Approaching the door, winded, her heart pounded a relentless drumbeat against her ribcage, both from fear and physical exertion. The door to Elena's flat opened before she could knock, revealing the young Latina girl—who couldn't be older than sixteen or seventeen—she assumed was Maria, the girl she'd spoken to on the phone. Her face was etched with lines of worry and relief at the same time.

The girl's silent greeting spoke volumes as to the gravity of the situation, and without a word, she closed the door and guided Luisa through the kitchen and down the hallway to Elena's room, each step heavy with foreboding.

Luisa entered the bedroom, giving a slight nod to Carrie, who stood at the foot of the bed, her hands crossed over her breasts, a sad and somber look blanketing her face. She stopped beside the woman, her daughter's best friend whom she'd never met, and placed a comforting hand on her shoulder.

"Thank you for being here for my daughter," Luisa said.

Carrie, moved by the gesture, let out a slight sob, then quickly covered her mouth with one hand.

Luisa gave her shoulder one more brief squeeze before navigating around the bed, where she stood silently for a long moment, looking down at Elena. The bathrobe, which had been hastily slipped on by Carrie and Maria, had fallen open slightly, revealing a portion of her left breast. Luisa adjusted the robe gently and cinching the belt more securely.

Elena's eyes were open, staring at the ceiling. The deep bruises around her neck resembled splayed fingers, as if she'd been strangled. Luisa's hands shook as she pushed back strands of Elena's hair, tucking both sides behind her ears. Tears, borne of fear, frustration, and a deep-seated maternal despair, streamed down her cheeks as she was confronted with the physical manifestation of her deepest fears. She hugged Elena for a long moment, her head pressed firmly against her daughter's slowly rising bosom, before leaning forward and kissing her cheeks.

"What happened?" Luisa asked, brushing tears from her cheeks. Her eyes remained locked on Elena's still form, searching for any sign of life in the stillness that enveloped her daughter.

"*Es difícil de explicar,*" (It's...it's hard to explain") Maria started.

Luisa, her back still to both Maria and Carrie,

said, "In English, so your friend can understand."

Maria glanced at Carrie, then back to Luisa. "We believe something has taken hold of Elena, something...not of this world." Maria's voice was a hesitant whisper.

"You found help?" Luisa asked. Her voice was firm, demanding.

"Yes, a priest," Carrie said. "Tomas. He's dealt with this sort of...affliction...before. He's preparing now and will be here soon." Her words, intended to comfort, instead stoked the flames of Luisa's fears, igniting memories of a battle fought in the shadows, a battle she had hoped her daughter would never have to face again.

Luisa turned to them, her gaze fraught with the weight of unspoken knowledge as it met Carrie's and Maria's. In their eyes, she saw the reflection of her own fear, the acknowledgment of a horror too daunting to name.

"This is no *affliction*. This is the devil's work. He's taken my child again," Luisa said.

Carrie's eyebrows raised. "What do you mean again?"

Luisa looked away, her eyes once more focusing on her daughter. She slid down from the edge of the bed onto her knees and retrieved a rosary from her sweater pocket. She held the rosary in her trembling hand, her fingers gliding across worn beads in a familiar, intimate manner. She crossed herself and kissed the cross before bowing her head against the mattress.

"*Señora*, please tell us what you mean," Maria said when Luisa did not answer Carrie's question. "This has happened before? Please, you must tell us," she implored, her voice gentle yet imbued with an urgency that Luisa felt resonate within her own fractured heart.

Torn between the instinctual desire to shield her daughter from the world's prying eyes and the acute awareness of the stakes at hand, Luisa found herself at a crossroads. To open the door to the past was to deepen the darkness she had fought so hard to escape. Yet the love for her daughter, a force more formidable than any fear, guided her decision. "I...I will tell you everything," she acquiesced, her resolve solidifying with each word. "Tomas must hear it, too, but I cannot bring myself to tell it twice."

The room, charged with a tense anticipation, fell silent, a quiet vigil held in the space between hope and despair. Luisa felt the weight of the past and present settle around her like an unbearable shroud. Her mind was a tumult of memories, each one a ghost from a past she had tried to leave behind. Yet, in this moment, beside her daughter, she found a semblance of courage, for she had defeated the devil before, and she would defeat him again.

Maria crossed the room and stood next to the kneeling woman and placed a hand on her shoulder. "There is something you should see."

Luisa finished her prayer, crossed herself again, then stood slowly using the bed for support. When she looked at Maria, her eyes were red and glassy.

"Maybe we shouldn't—" Carrie started.

"Show me," Luisa said firmly.

She followed Maria to the closet, watching the young girl carefully. She had a steel within her that Luisa respected. She reminded her very much of her dear Elena.

The girl pulled the door open, stepped into the darkness, and turned on the light. Luisa, standing at the threshold of the closet, immediately saw the dark tendrils, like hundreds of tentacles spreading their way across the ceiling.

"*Dios mio*," Luisa said, again crossing herself. She grabbed Maria's arm, pulling her urgently out of the closet before closing the door.

As they awaited Tomas's arrival, the room seemed to contract, the walls echoing back their collective anxiety and the unspoken fears. Luisa returned to Elena's side, a silent guardian whispering prayers of deliverance in anticipation of the battle ahead.

TWENTY-ONE

TOMAS STOOD AT THE THRESHOLD OF THE APARTMENT. He wore a black cassock beneath a slightly aged white surplice. A long purple stole hung around his neck, which he adjusted slightly. His attire was a stark transformation from the casual wear he'd wore earlier. He emanated an aura of grave determination that almost immediately set each of the gathered women at ease. He carried with him a battered leather case, darkened with age and use, which he set on the kitchen island.

Luisa stepped forward, her hand stretched in front of her. "Hello, Tomas, I am Luisa. Elena's mother."

Accepting her hand, Tomas clasped it gently. "I

know this is a difficult time for you," he said. His gaze shifted from Luis to Carrie and Maria. "For all of you."

"Thank you for coming," Maria said, now standing beside Luisa. She hooked her arm through Luisa's in a show of support and comfort, for which Luisa was grateful.

"Of course." A moment of silence passed. "Bring me to her," Tomas finally said, his eyes surveying the room, as if looking for something.

"This way," Maria said.

Upon entering Elena's room, his gaze swept across the space, again as if searching for something, finally resting on the woman on the bed. Without a word, he crossed the room and sat on the edge of the bed. He crossed himself and then made the sign of the cross over Elena before leaning forward to examine her in the dim light of the room. He noted the deep bruises around her throat and dry blood just inside the flare of her nostrils. He also noticed the foul stench of decay on her breath.

Standing, he turned to find the trio of women huddled at the doorway watching him with a mixture of fear and anticipation in their eyes. It was a look he'd seen many times on the faces of the families of the afflicted across the many exorcisms he'd performed in his tenure with the church. Soon their expressions would be that of terror.

He fixed his gaze on the closet door and strode across the room. His hand rested on the knob momentarily before he twisted it and pulled the door open. The light was still on. Having seen the photos on Maria's phone, he thought he knew what to expect. Yet seeing it with his own eyes evoked an immediate sense of pure evil.

The Catholic Church, with its long history of exorcisms, taught that demons could manipulate the physical environment as a means to instill fear, confusion, and despair among the living. This fungus was not a biological anomaly; it was a symbol, a physical manifestation of the corruption and decay. The fungus, growing and spreading so quickly, was a metaphor for the insidious nature of this evil—slowly spreading, almost imperceptibly, until it entrenched itself deeply within the home and, by extension, Elena.

Closing the door, Tomas looked at the women, his expression solemn. "Let's talk outside," he suggested.

In the kitchen, they gathered around the island.

"There is something I must tell you before you begin," Luisa said, her voice a fragile thread in the tense air.

Tomas nodded, signaling for Luisa to continue.

"Twenty-two years ago, we lived in Ecuador, in the small rural city of Alausi," Luisa said. She pulled out one of the stools and sat, resting her arms against the cool countertop. She interlaced her fingers, the rosary nestled between her rough hands. "Elena was five years old. Her birthday was two days before, but we celebrated on the weekend, invited the whole family."

Luisa paused, her eyes fixed on her hands and the rosary clutched between them. "That day of celebration ended in horror for my Elena. On that day, the devil took her."

Maria and Carrie both gasped in unison.

"My family is cursed," Luisa said matter-of-factly. "My mother and brother, Milton, were both taken by the devil before my Elena. My mother was a tarot reader who deeply believed in the spirit world and used the cards for malicious reasons, to manipulate others and to seek revenge, opening herself to the evil. Milton was a caregiver at a mental health service for the elderly. He darkened his soul with despicable, vile acts with an old woman who was mentally disabled. Then the evil took Elena, an innocent child."

Tomas listened intently, piecing together the lineage of darkness that had plagued their family. "The origin of such entities often lies in actions that open doors best left closed," he said.

"I can understand something like this happening to Luisa's mother and brother," Carrie said. "But why Elena? Why an innocent child?"

"Demonic entities are drawn to the innocent, seeing them as easier targets to manipulate and control. It's speculated that children lack the mental and spiritual defenses necessary to resist possession. The appeal of corrupting the innocent is very appealing to the fallen angels and tempters."

They all fell silent, each processing, trying to wrap their heads around the situation.

Tomas shifted the conversation toward the imminent exorcism. "What we're facing is not just about Elena; it's about confronting a darkness that has latched onto your family across generations," he explained, his tone grave.

He proceeded to outline the rules, each directive underscored with a severity designed to impress upon them the gravity of their situation. "During the exorcism, it's imperative that you do not engage with Elena directly. The demon will use her voice to lie, to manipulate. Remember, it's not Elena speaking but the entity that's taken hold of her."

Tomas's instructions were clear, his demeanor unyielding. "Never be alone in the room with her. The demon seeks isolation to weaken us. Stay vigilant, adhere to prayer, and follow my lead without hesitation."

The air in the kitchen was thick with a tension that mirrored the seriousness of Tomas's words. It was as if he intended to frighten them, a tactic to ensure their unwavering attention and compliance.

"Do you all understand? This is not merely a ritual; it's a battle for Elena's soul, and by extension, the sanctity of your family," Tomas emphasized, seeking an acknowledgment from each person present.

One by one, they voiced their understanding, a chorus of commitment in the face of the unknown. Tomas then led them in a prayer, anointing each with holy oil, a symbolic gesture of protection and blessing.

As they prepared to return to Elena's side, the

night seemed to press in around them, a tangible darkness against the light of their resolve. Tomas's final glance before leaving the kitchen was one of a man braced for the storm, a leader ready to guide his flock through the valley of the shadow of death.

Twenty-Two

Tomas walked the perimeter of the bedroom slowly, moving around furniture that flanked the walls, sprinkling holy water in a clockwise direction. The act symbolized cleansing the space of any negative energies and creating a sacred area for the ritual. After, he retrieved small white candles—each with a gold cross stamped into them—from his bag and blessed with a prayer. He handed one to Carrie, Maria, and Luisa, kept one for himself. He directed them to place their candles in each of the four corners of the room, creating a symbolic barrier against evil.

From the patinated leather case, Tomas withdrew four padded restraints. Each cuff was made from a durable neoprene-like material surrounded by thick leather. One stainless steel ring was sewn into each cuff, from which a leather belt extended. The belts could be fashioned around bedposts or chair arms and legs, securing the possessed.

With his back to the group, he called for Carrie to join him. She stood nervously beside him. Holding two of the restraints out to her, Tomas said, "Please help me restrain Elena."

Carrie stared at the restraints for several seconds before hesitantly accepting them. Cautiously, she asked, "Are these really necessary?"

"Yes," Tomas said, gently but firmly. "For her safety and our own."

Following Tomas to the bedside, Carrie set both of the restraints on the bed between Elena's legs, then picked up one and examined it briefly, familiarizing herself with its function. She loosened the leather flap that fastened the cuff, then spread the cuff open, keeping it spread with her fingers. Starting with Elena's left foot, Carrie lifted it gently, several inches off the bed, just high enough to slip the restraint below before gently setting her ankle within. She fumbled a bit with the leather strap as she secured it with the small buckle.

"Make sure it's tight," Tomas said, peering at her from the other side of the bed. His brown eyes fixed on hers. "She mustn't be able to break free from them."

Carrie nodded. She finished securing the restraint around Elena's ankle, then tugged at it firmly until she was satisfied it would hold. She looked at Tomas for approval. He nodded and went on with his work.

Taking the remaining restraint, Carrie moved to the head of the bed. She knelt so she was level with the mattress, then leaned across Elena to grasp her left arm, which laid limply across her abdomen. Carried gently guided her arm into place with her hand slightly above her head and near the base of the headboard.

Following the same process, Carrie slipped Elena's wrist into the restraint, securing it firmly with the leather strap. As she wrapped the longer strap around the frame of the headboard, she glanced at Elena. Her head had shifted to the left and her eyes, vacant and lifeless moments ago, flickered with a sudden spark. A chilling glint replaced the emptiness, followed by a slow, sinister smile that spread across her face. It wasn't a human expression; it was a predator's smirk, devoid of warmth and full of malice.

Carrie sucked in her breath in a sudden gasp and

pushed back, landing on her ass and sliding back a few feet from the bed. Her heart thudded in her chest and a tingling heat rose in her esophagus and into her cheeks.

She looked at Tomas, her breath quickening in her lungs. He was securing Elena's right wrist with the padded restraint, his attention focused on his task. Maria and Luisa stood behind Carrie, near the bureau where Tomas had set his leather bag. The two women, old and young, stared blankly at her, both seemingly oblivious to what Carrie had just witnessed.

Tomas, having secured Elena with the restraints, crossed the room and retrieved a Bible and crucifix from his bag. The crucifix glimmered in the candlelight as he walked toward Carrie and Elena. He placed the crucifix on the nightstand, beside Elena's head, then took his place at the foot of the bed.

"He cannot protect you," Elena said, drawing Carrie's attention. The sinister smirk still spread across her face, sending shivers down Carrie's spine.

With a deep breath, Tomas began. "In the name of the Father, and of the Son, and of the Holy Spirit. Amen."

In the dimly lit room, shadows danced, flickering

across the walls. Carrie was frozen, her gaze locked on Elena, or rather the entity that had taken residence within her friend. The air was thick, charged with an electric sense of dread that clawed at Carrie's nerves as she realized the demon had targeted her, somehow isolating her from the attention of the others.

"Almighty and Everlasting God," Tomas continued, "who didst create man in Thine Own Image, and didst grant him dominion over all the works of Thy hands, look with favor upon this Thy servant Elena, who is grievously oppressed by the power of the evil one."

Suddenly, the room seemed to warp, as though the flicking shadows somehow opened a portal to a nightmare realm. The once-familiar setting of Elena's bedroom twisted into a grotesque caricature of itself. Carrie's heart hammered more relentlessly in her chest as the demon, wearing Elena's face like a grotesque mask, spoke.

"Carrie," it hissed, its voice a sickening blend of Elena's and something far darker. "Do you see what they all really think of you?"

"By the authority which Thou hast given unto Thy Church, and in the Name of Thy Blessed Son, our Lord Jesus Christ, I command thee, unclean spirit, whoever thou art, to depart from this Thy creature, and to return from whence thou camest."

Before Carrie could respond, the room dissolved into a nightmarish classroom. Her students' faces, twisted in disdain, sneered at her from the darkness. Elena, standing amongst them, laughed mockingly. "You're a worthless bitch," they chanted, their words slicing through Carrie like knives. "A useless child-woman who sucks the teat of her father's chest. A weak, despicable twat who can't stand on her own merits."

Carrie reached out, desperate for any sign of reality, but her hands grasped only air.

"May the most holy Name of Jesus, before Whom every knee doth bend, both of things in heaven, and things on earth, and things under the earth, be to thee a terror and a scourge. May the sign of the holy Cross, which the wicked spirits dread, be thy punishment."

The vision shifted, and Carrie found herself standing in the ruins of her home. Documents floated around her, decrees of bankruptcy, foreclosure notices, her life's comfort and security stripped away. A voice, cruel and taunting, whispered of her father's disappointment, of a scandal that had left her name tarnished and her pockets empty.

"Alone and penniless, Carrie," it sneered. "You'll be turned out on the streets, destitute, reduced to sucking cock for a buck."

"May the power of the Blessed Virgin Mary, Mother of God, conceived without sin, ever Virgin, be thy downfall. May the prayers of the blessed Saints Michael, Raphael, Gabriel, and all the holy Angels, and of all the Saints of God, be thy confusion and defeat."

The scene morphed yet again, this time into an endless void. Calls for help echoed back unanswered. Silhouettes of Tomas, Maria, and Luisa passed by, their eyes glancing through her as if she were a ghost. Elena's shadow turned away, leaving Carrie in a darkness so complete it threatened to swallow her whole.

"Forgotten, by everyone," the demon whispered. "You're meaningless, a burden, completely unforgettable. No one wants you. You're better off dead. You should kill yourself."

"Depart, then, accursed spirit, and give place to the Holy Spirit. Flee from the presence of the Living God, from the True and Holy Cross, from the Virgin Mary, Mother of God, from all the holy Angels and Saints. Mayest thou have no power henceforth, neither place nor influence in this servant of God."

A mirror materialized in the void, its surface rippling like water. Carrie, compelled by a force she couldn't resist, looked into it. Her reflection twisted, aging decades in moments, skin sagging, eyes hollowing. Then her face contorted, becoming monstrous, unrecognizable.

"This is what you truly are," the demon's voice echoed, a mockery of comfort. "A lecherous hag!"

"This I command thee, Satan, in the Name of the Father, and of the Son, and of the Holy Spirit. Amen."

As quickly as they had appeared, the visions shattered, leaving Carrie gasping for breath on the cold floor, her fingers gripping the nap of the carpet so intensely her tendons of her wrists ached and burned. The room was again as it had been. Tomas, Maria, and Luisa, oblivious to her torment, whispered prayers, their voices a constant drone. Elena's body, controlled by the demon, turned away, its laughter echoing in Carrie's mind long after it had stopped.

TWENTY-THREE

MARIA STOOD AT THE THRESHOLD OF HELL, NOT ONE wrought in fire and brimstone, but one that whispered her name with a familiarity that chilled her to the bone. The air in Elena's room, thick with the scent of incense and palpable fear, seemed to constrict around her, a tangible force intent on squeezing the secrets from her. She had entered this room armed with faith and a desire to help Elena, but now, she found herself facing an adversary that knew her more intimately than any confidante ever could.

"Eternal God, source of all light and goodness, cast Your merciful gaze upon this child of Yours, Elena Vera, who lies bound by the chains of darkness," Tomas's voice resounded across the room, reverberating off the walls as though from surround sound speakers mounted in every corner. "Remember the promise You made, O Lord, to be close to the brokenhearted and to deliver those who cry out to You in their distress."

The demon, cloaked in Elena's tortured form, turned its gaze upon Maria, its eyes gleaming with a malevolent light. "Maria, sweet Maria," it cooed, its voice a vile parody of affection, "do you think your desires are hidden? Your heart screams your secrets, louder than any prayer you could whisper."

"By the authority vested in me by Your Holy Church, and empowered by the unwavering faith of Your people gathered here, I command you, foul spirit, to manifest yourself and declare your name."

Maria's breath hitched, her eyes darting to the others in the room. Tomas, his voice steady as he recited the prayers, Luisa, and the others, all enveloped in their own battle, were oblivious to the demon's cruel assault on her psyche.

"You are in love with me," Elena said and smiled. "You don't think I know? I've seen you stalking my Instagram while you're in class, bookmarking the photos of me in a bikini to your favorites so you can touch moist pussy at night."

"That's not true!" Maria yelled, her face growing

flush with the rising heat of embarrassment at the verbalization of her deepest desires.

"Begone, creature of malice! Flee before the radiant light of the Holy Cross, symbol of our Lord Jesus Christ's victory over sin and death. May the Sacred Name of Jesus, whispered by angels and revered by men, pierce through your darkness and expel you from this sacred space."

The demon's voice slithered through the air, detailing obscene acts, desecrating Maria's unspoken feelings for Elena with every crude word. "At night, you dream of us, you naughty, filthy child, tangled in passionate lust."

"May the Blessed Virgin Mary, Mother of God, whose purity and unwavering faith vanquished the serpent of old, be your bane. May the intercession of Saint Michael, the valiant defender of the heavenly host, and all the holy angels and saints, be your undoing."

"You like the taste of my dripping pussy on your tongue," Elena croaked. "You probe my ass with your nasty little fingers before sticking them into your own slutty little snatch, you vile child!"

"Depart, malevolent spirit! Leave this vessel of God and return to the abyss from whence you came. May you have no power, influence, or hold over this soul. This I command, in the name of the Father, and of the Son, and of the Holy Spirit. Amen."

"Imagine the scandal, Maria. The disgust. The rejection, when they all find out you're a nasty little slut that's hot for teacher!" it sneered, twisting her deepest desires into grotesque caricatures. The room felt hotter, the walls inching closer, as if the very house conspired to trap Maria with her fears.

Panic surged through Maria, a tidal wave of fear that threatened to sweep her away, out to a raging sea. She turned, a desperate need to flee filling her, to escape the exposure, the judgment, the retched demon. But before she could take more than a few steps, Carrie was there to halt her.

"Maria, it's lies!" Carrie's voice was firm, her hands grasping Maria's with a strength that belied her appearance. "Don't listen to it. Whatever it said, whatever it showed you, it's not real. It wants to isolate us, to break us down. Don't give in to it."

Maria's breath came in short, ragged gasps. Her eyes locked with Carrie's, and in them she found a flicker of understanding, a shared acknowledgment of the horror they faced but also a resolve that lent her strength.

With a shaky exhale, Maria allowed Carrie to pull her close, their foreheads pressed together as they turned back to face the demon. Together, they began to pray, their voices a soft counterpoint to the cacophony of the demon's ranting. The words of the Hail Mary were a lifeline, pulling Maria back from the precipice of despair.

As they prayed, the demon's voice faded, its power waning in the face of their united front. Maria still felt the echo of its words, a lingering shadow eclipsing her heart, but in this moment, she was not alone. Carrie's presence, the warmth of her hand in her own, was a tangible reminder that together, they could face the darkness. Overcome.

Twenty-Four

THE ROSARY BEADS FELT LIKE ICE AGAINST LUISA'S sweating palms, each whispered prayer a futile dam against the tide of terror surging through her. A strangled cry pierced the room, tearing Luisa's gaze from her desperate prayers. Maria's face contorted into a mask of fear and shame. Tears streamed down her cheeks as she tried to flee.

The devil was doing its work.

Luisa's heart hammered against her ribs, a frantic drum solo against the backdrop of the priest's booming voice. "The Lord is my light and my salvation; whom shall I fear? The Lord is the strength of my life; of whom shall I be afraid?"

Carrie, eyes wide with fear, knelt beside Maria,

their hands clasped in a desperate plea for solace, as they recited the Lord's Prayer in unison. Across the room, Tomas stood, a fierce warrior brandishing holy weapons—Bible and crucifix held aloft like shields against the encroaching darkness. He switched the Bible to the hand that held the crucifix. In the other, he wielded the vial of holy water, flicking his wrist as he made the sign of the cross.

Tomas's voice rose, echoing with conviction. "We come in the name of the Father, who created all that is, and in the name of the Son, who conquered death itself. We come in the name of the Holy Spirit, who resides within each of us, a beacon of hope in the face of despair."

The blessed liquid singed Elena's skin, and she screamed. Her body began to thud rapidly against the bed as it was wracked with tremors.

The room seemed to pulse with a sinister energy, and Luisa's prayers became more fervent, a desperate plea for salvation.

"*Ayúdame, Mami. ¡Duele, duele mucho!*" ("Help me, Mommy. It hurts, it hurts so bad!")

The voice, sweet and innocent, ripped through the cacophony of terror like a beacon in the storm. Luisa whipped her head toward the source—and her blood ran cold.

There, on the bed, lay Elena. A small, frail child, her body contorted in agony, her skin marred by the demon's touch. But her eyes, though filled with pain, were undeniably her daughter's.

Luisa's breath hitched. This wasn't a possessed child anymore. This was a demon, given flesh and form through her own flesh and blood. Panic choked her, a primal urge to claw her way out of her own skin, clawing at her sanity.

A wave of nausea washed over Luisa. The demon toyed with them, twisted reality, fueled their fear. She knew this to be true. She had to be strong, for Elena. To deny it, to ignore it. A cold fury replaced the terror gripping her heart. She wouldn't let this entity win. Not her daughter.

"Help me, Mommy! It burns!"

Luisa clawed at her ears, fingernails digging into flesh in a desperate attempt to silence the beast. Elena's voice, no longer human, pulsed in her head, like a pressure building behind her eyes that threatened to split her head asunder. The air itself seemed to vibrate with the banshee's shriek, a rising tide of pure agony that threatened to drown her. Legs buckling beneath the psychic assault, Luisa lurched to her feet, a marionette puppet jerked by unseen strings. Her gait, a grotesque parody of a walk, propelled her toward the source of the torment.

Carrie's voice, laced with raw terror, sliced through the maddening din. "Luisa, no!" But the warning fell on deaf ears, lost in the tempestuous sea of sound and fury consuming Luisa.

Luisa stumbled. Her legs, jelly under the weight of fear and anguish, refused to hold her. She fell, scraping her knees raw on the rough fabric of the carpet. Ignoring the searing pain, she crawled toward the bed, a primal need to protect her child overriding the screams that filled her head. As Luisa reached the bed, she saw Tomas raise the crucifix, its holy symbol glowing with an otherworldly light. His voice boomed, a weapon against the darkness.

"But know this," Tomas continued, his voice loud and firm, "we come not just with faith, but with a righteous fury. You have dared to invade the sacred space of a human soul, and for that, you will face the full wrath of God's love. You will be banished, cast back into the abyss from whence you came, never to return."

The child Elena's face was covered with black ooze that leaked from its rent flesh. One eye stared at Luisa, terror-stricken. Luisa touched Elena's face, even as Carrie and Maria yelled for her to get away.

Suddenly, Elena's mouth stretched impossibly wide, revealing rows of razor-sharp teeth. A scream, inhuman and horrifying, ripped from her throat as she lunged toward Luisa.

Tomas raised a crucifix, the symbol of Christ's sacrifice glinting in the dim light. "This symbol, a testament to the ultimate triumph over evil, shall be your undoing. Begone, foul spirit! Flee before the light and return to the darkness from which you were spawned. This vessel you have corrupted is no longer yours to claim."

Agony lanced through Luisa's arm as three of her fingers vanished into the maw of the possessed child. She screamed, a primal cry of pain and terror. Strong hands pulled her back, tearing her away from the monstrosity on the bed.

Maria shouted, her lips emphasizing her words, but Luisa could only hear Elena's evil, booming laugh. Luisa screamed, her voice shrill and piercing. Maria slapped Luisa's face hard, then again when Luisa continued to scream.

"It's not real! It's not real!" Maria's voice cut through the fog clouding Luisa's thoughts. "Look at me, Luisa! You must resist! You must pray!"

"¡Mis dedos!"("My fingers!") Luisa yelled and held up her hand in front of her to show the girl.

Instead of blood and stumps, all her fingers were attached; her hand was whole. Luisa slumped against Maria, the world blurring around her. She sobbed uncontrollably, the phantom pain in her hand throbbing in her mind.

TWENTY-FIVE

ELENA'S CONSCIOUSNESS HUNG SUSPENDED IN A BLACK, superheated void. The air, thick as molasses, pulsed with a sickening rhythm that throbbed through her veins, every nerve, every muscle, and every fiber of her being. A neurotic chorus of whispers scratched at the edge of her awareness like nails against a chalkboard in the hollow chamber of her besieged mind.

Something stirred in the ether, a vile, blasphemous presence taking shape in the depths. With a jolt of horror, Elena recognized the monstrosity. *La vieja malvada.* Her tattered hospital gown hung like rotting flesh on a skeletal frame, matted white hair swirling around her mottled, cracked face. Her eyes, pools of liquid mercury, locked onto Elena with a predatory hunger.

"Mine," the hag hissed, her voice like shards of ice scraped across bone. "You belong to me. You've always belonged to me."

A frigid terror seized Elena's heart. She tried to scream, to force words from her throat, but the sound died, trapped in the suffocating, cloying emptiness.

The old woman lunged, gnarled hands extended with razor-sharp nails. The stench of decay washed over Elena, making her gag. She willed herself to move, to fight, but her body, a distant husk on some faraway floor, did not obey.

Pain ripped through her like a thousand knives. Invisible claws raked through her mind, tearing apart her thoughts, her memories, her very sense of self. Each scrape brought a surge of new whispers, vile and insidious, promising darkness and despair, destroying any hope of salvation. Claws slashed into the raw wounds, festering, turning her own mind against her.

Tears streamed down Elena's face, silent and unseen in the void of the abyss of whispers. The evil woman cackled, a sound that reverberated through her very being, each note a spike of raw agony.

"Weak!" the beast boomed, its voice echoing like thunder through the cavernous void. "Pathetic! This struggle is a mere plaything to me. You will crumble like dry leaves beneath my foot. You will surrender your will, as all must, and I will claim you utterly!"

The hag's skeletal fingers tightened around Elena's essence, squeezing and twisting, the pressure growing unbearable. Elena felt something inside her snap, a brittle thread of her sanity unraveling. In the distance, she heard Tomas's voice, faintly, but it seemed worlds away—useless against the horror consuming her.

As the suffocating darkness threatened to claim her mind, a flicker ignited within Elena. Not a roaring inferno, but a single, defiant ember. It sputtered against the encroaching shadows, fueled by a sliver of her spirit that refused to be extinguished. Fragile, yes, but it was hers. It was a primal scream of defiance etched upon the very fabric of her being.

The hag recoiled, the chilling screech of a thwarted predator ripping through the cacophony of whispers. "You dare resist?" she hissed, her voice dripping with venomous delight. "So be it, little ember. You will only make the breaking all the more exquisite."

La vieja malvada's grip tightened, a vice around

Elena's spirit, twisting until the pain threatened to shatter her sanity. With a gasp, Elena clung to that defiant spark, willing it to bloom, to become a roaring inferno against the encroaching darkness. It felt like a single candle flickering against a hurricane, a puny, flickering thing, but it was all she had.

From the world beyond the void, a faint echo of chanting prayer seeped through, a desperate plea cutting through the storm of whispers that gnawed at her mind. Elena strained toward it, each syllable a lifeline, a fragile barrier against the hag's insidious assault.

The hag seethed, her form contorting, morphing into a grotesque canvas of nightmare. She lunged once more, the stench of decay and malice a physical assault. Elena braced herself, the spark flickering precariously as the hag's claws reached out, poised to snuff it out forever.

Twenty-Six

THE ROOM VIBRATED WITH A MALEVOLENT RUMBLE AS if the walls were alive. A moaning and grinding sound resonated around the room, as if they were in the metal hull of a submarine, slowly being crushed by intense pressure. A crack appeared in the wall above the bed, and black steam store through its opening with a hissing and whining sound.

Elena writhed on the bed, a grotesque marionette controlled by unseen strings, aggressively rattling the restraints that bound her to the bed. Her eyes, now pools of soulless black, rolled up until only the whites showed, settling on Tomas's in a terrifying challenge.

"*Vade retro, Satanas!*" Tomas roared, his voice hoarse from hours of desperate prayer. The crucifix trembled in his hand, the silver seeming to tarnish in the presence of the wretched entity.

Elena's smile, a grotesque parody of human joy, revealed teeth decayed and worn, oozing foul black liquid from diseased gums. A thick mass of flies gathered above her head, a twister of angry insects, their incessant buzzing a harsh drone that assaulted the ears, confusing the senses.

"Foolish priest," it rasped in a voice that sounded like a chorus of tortured souls. "You cannot banish what you cannot comprehend. You are but a gnat challenging a hurricane."

Before Tomas's eyes, Elena's twisted form molted, contracted, reformed, as if she were a clay model on a sculptor's block. Upon the bed, arms and legs stretched out to each of the four corners by the restraints, lay the boy. He lifted his head, locking eyes with Tomas. Veins, like thin, black tendrils, crept across his pale skin, pulsating with an other-worldly force. His lips were drawn back in a snarl, revealing teeth that seemed too sharp, too eager. Every feature was exaggerated, contorted by the sinister entity within, transforming the child's visage.

"Guillermo..." Tomas choked the boy's name from his parched throat.

"Playing God again, you pathetic fool?" the boy snarled. His voice, though belonging to a child, held the malice of a thousand hells.

Tomas stumbled back, the boy's words a sucker punch to his gut.

"Missed me, haven't you, priest?" Guillermo cooed, his voice dripping with venom. "It's your fault I'm burning in hell. You were too weak, too pathetic, too scared to save me."

The crucifix in Tomas's hand felt like lead. He squeezed it tighter, knuckles turning white, forcing the words out through a throat choked with grief and guilt. "Silence, demon! Begone from this vessel!"

The boy's smile stretched wider, revealing rows of needle-sharp teeth. "Oh, but I am the vessel, you senile fool. This woman is just a plaything. And you, you're just a joke. Just like you were to me."

A wave of nausea washed over Tomas. The memory of young Guillermo's lifeless body, the embarrassment of the canonical trial that resulted in his excommunication, the suffocating weight of his own failure and the tragic loss of Guillermo's life and soul, were drowning him. He squeezed his eyes shut, a sob escaping his lips.

"Pathetic," the boy spat, his voice dripping with disgust. "You couldn't save me, and you can't save her. You'll just watch her rot from the inside out, just like you watched me."

Across the room, Carrie clutched Maria's hands, their foreheads pressed together, eyes squeezed tightly shut. Maria led their prayers, raising her voice to compete against the rumbling walls, the drone of the flies, and steam of hellfire. "... HALLOWED BE THY NAME. THY KINGDOM COME. THY WILL BE DONE..."

Luisa pressed her rosary to her lips, whispering fervent prayers. Sweat ran from her temples, tears from her eyes. The sound of thousands of flies buzzing swelled and overwhelmed the room. Luisa's prayers faltered. She opened her eyes to a horrifying sight. A thick cloud of flies poured from the fissure in the wall above the bed, massing in a swarming funnel above Elena. Without warning, the mass attacked Tomas, bringing him to his knees.

Her eyes blazing with a mother's fierce love, Luisa pushed up from the floor and stumbled to the dresser, falling against it, grasping at it to keep her balance. The sturdy piece of furniture vibrated against her palms. She felt the drone of the flies in the soles of her feet, as if they were beneath the floor. She pawed at Tomas's leather bag and snatched a vial of holy water from within. Pulling the small white cap from the mouth of the vessel, Luisa gripped the vial tightly. The drone of the flies increased, attacking her eardrums, throwing off her equilibrium. Her stomach rose, and she felt nauseous. She staggered toward the bed, her hand raised high above her head, her arm arching down to splash the blessed liquid.

"Get away from me, foul creature!" Elena yelled, her voice cracking with defiance. With the flick of her head, she sent Luisa flying across the room, her frail body slamming against the wall near the bathroom where she lay crumpled and dazed.

With a speed defying human limitations, the possessed body tore away from its restraints as if they were made of paper rings created by a child and hurled itself at Luisa. A guttural roar filled the room, opening cracks across the walls, the stench of brimstone and buzzing pestilence following in its wake.

Carrie and Maria started toward Luisa, fear burning in their stomachs like acid. The carpet came alive below their feet, the wool filaments sprouting like angry arms of kelp, winding around their feet and ankles, entwining their knees, rooting them in place.

Luisa screamed, squeezed her eyes shut, protecting them from the mass of flies. She swung her arm wildly, batting at the thing that was not her daughter. The holy water flew from the vial, sizzling on Elena's face like acid, drawing a bloodcurdling shriek that echoed through the walls, warping them, pressing them out as if something behind were trying to burst from within. The demon recoiled, its infernal fury momentarily eclipsed by the searing agony.

Seizing this fleeting opportunity, Tomas regained his composure and launched into the Latin rite. "*Te increpo et adjuro, omnis immundus spiritus...*" The words, imbued with ancient power, resonated through the room, vibrating in the very air.

"*Non potes me vincere! Ego sum legio, et ego multi!*" ("You cannot defeat me! I am Legion, and I am many!") it roared, the voice shaking the very foundations of the room.

Suddenly, the crucifix clutched in Tomas's hand grew searing hot. He screamed, flinging it across the room, where it clattered against the wall and burst into flames. The metal singed the carpet, and Luisa slapped at the flames before the whole carpet ignited.

"*See?*" the demon taunted, its voice dripping with venomous glee. "Your God has abandoned you."

The closet door burst open, a blast of superheated air knocking Tomas to his knees and pushing the women back against the walls. The room shook thunderously, and the furniture began to rattle rapidly. Candles extinguished. Everything that was not heavy or solid was sucked up into the air all around the room, caught in the eye of hell's tornado.

Elena stood, her arms stretched out wide, a grotesque parody of Christ's crucifixion. A terrifying roar loosed from her chest as her body began to twist and writhe, expand and contract, the flesh roiling. Half her face twisted in on itself, seemed to churn like molten lava, growing in size until it blended with the face of *la vieja malvada*.

Her body doubled in size, her mottled flesh bulging, tearing through the thin layer of the decrepit fabric of her clothing. *La vieja malvada* stretched her mouth wide, like the unhinged jaw of a viper. The snake tongue lashed out, wrapping around Luisa's neck. The tongue began to rescind, with the speed of a retracting measuring tape, dragging her toward the beast.

Carrie grasped Luisa's arm and held fast against the force of the blast and the droning flies. Furniture dislodged and flew across the room. The desk slid across the carpet in as if it weight nothing and pinned Maria against the wall from mid-thigh down.

A chair struck Tomas's head, drawing blood and knocking him backward.

The tendrils of demon goo began to spread from the closet, hundreds of black feelers grasping the door frame, slithering along the walls, across the carpet. The foul limbs grasped Tomas, began to drag him toward the closet. The fungus reached Maria, enveloping her. She felt it clamping her throat, at the corners of her lips, across her teeth, her tongue. It slithered up Carrie's legs, her arms, pulling her to the carpet, immobilizing her like a fly trapped in a spider's cocooned web. She lost her grip on Luisa, and the frail woman was dragged across the room into the awaiting arms of *la vieja malvada*.

Tomas fought fiercely, digging his feet into the deep nap of the carpet, grasping for purchase with one hand, wielding the Bible in the other. He shouted, "IN THE NAME OF JESUS CHRIST, I COMMAND YOU TO FLEE. 'AT THE NAME OF JESUS EVERY KNEE SHOULD BOW, IN HEAVEN AND ON EARTH AND UNDER THE EARTH.'" The words thundered from his throat with such force his vocal cords tore, leaving him voiceless.

Suddenly, a tremor ran through the room, a deep vibration that resonated in Tomas's bones. The air crackled, charged with an unseen energy. The fetid stench of evil receded, replaced by a faint, ozone tang.

He squeezed his eyes shut, bracing for the inevitable. But instead of the searing pain of oblivion, a warmth, unlike anything he'd ever known, blossomed in his chest. It spread outward, chasing away the cold dread, replacing it with a profound sense of peace.

He dared to open his eyes.

A light.

It wasn't a gentle luminescence, but a blazing inferno contained within Tomas, like a star gone supernova, birthing a radiance that eclipsed the sun in its intensity. The tendrils that gripped him sizzled, turned to ash, dissolving into wisps of smoke that danced on the edge of annihilation.

The room pulsed with the heartbeat of creation. Carrie, Maria, Luisa—all bathed in the ethereal glow—felt a peace descend upon them, a serenity deeper than any earthly slumber. Tears streamed down their faces, not of fear, but of a love so profound it brought them to their knees.

The brilliance dimmed, revealing a silhouette etched against the celestial fire. A figure of pure energy, radiating a power that humbled mountains and bowed galaxies. Time seemed to stutter, the very air pregnant with anticipation.

Then, a voice.

It wasn't a booming pronouncement, nor a whisper lost on the wind. It was a presence, a feeling that resonated within their very souls. A voice that spoke of love that conquered all, of sacrifice that redeemed the world.

"Fear not, Tomas, for I am with you."

The words echoed through the room, washing away the scars of trauma, leaving behind an unshakeable faith. Tomas, tears blurring his vision, turned to face the source of the voice. He saw no face, only the blinding radiance, yet he knew. He knew with a certainty that transcended reason that it was Him. The embodiment of hope. The bringer of light. Jesus Christ.

As the celestial glow faded, leaving behind a soft, comforting luminescence, Tomas rose. He was no longer the broken priest, haunted by failure. He was a vessel, forever touched by the divine.

The voice spoke again, this time through Tomas's ruined vocal cords, its tone filled with power that was undeniable and final.

"THIS VESSEL BELONGS TO THE LIGHT. BEGONE, CREATURE OF DARKNESS, AND

RETURN TO THE ABYSS FROM WHENCE YOU CAME!"

A brilliant white pulse of pure energy erupted from Tomas, as if his entire body were a weapon of the Lord. All but Tomas averted their eyes from the glorious brilliance, as powerful as the flare of the sun. A tidal wave of celestial energy slammed against the monstrous form of *la vieja malvada*.

It shrieked, a sound that curdled the blood and scraped against the soul. Her twisted limbs writhed as if in the grip of an invisible vise. The fetid ichor that oozed from her flesh bubbled and evaporated, replaced by a sickly luminescence that fought against the encroaching light.

It was a battle between corruption and purity, darkness and dawn. But the outcome was never in doubt. The light pressed in, relentless and unforgiving. The crone's form began to waver, the monstrous visage dissolving like a grotesque sculpture melting in the sun.

Her screams turned into a choked gurgle, the inhuman power that had fueled her fading with every passing moment. Slowly, agonizingly, she shrank, the darkness within her essence consumed by the holy radiance. When the light receded, Elena lay still, her pale face drained of color.

Silence descended upon the room, thick and heavy. Slowly, Tomas moved to the bed and looked at the young woman lying peacefully. Relief and exhaustion warred within him, leaving him numb.

He had not driven out the demon, but he had been a part of something greater, an instrument of a divine will.

As the first rays of dawn painted the sky, casting long shadows through the room, Tomas looked at the others. Tears welled up in his eyes, a mixture of relief and gratitude. They had faced the darkness together, and in that shared struggle, they had found a strength they never knew they possessed.

Luisa, her arms wrapped protectively around her daughter, looked at Tomas. "Thank you," she whispered, her voice thick with emotion.

Tomas simply nodded, unable to speak.

Epilogue

Two weeks had crawled by since the ordeal, and things had finally started to fall back into a normal groove for Elena. She met with a psychologist recommended by the teacher's union to satisfy the requirements to return to work. She stayed far away from the truth, obviously, and instead focused on her botched relationship with Natalie and how that had taken an emotional toll on her. Last week was her first week back, and she realized just how much she missed the classroom and her students.

Today, Elena sat behind her desk, hunched over a mountain of ungraded essays she assigned after the kids finished watching *The Outsiders*. She slowly worked her way through them and was only halfway done. She'd assigned the topic, *Outsiders in Your Own*

World: Identify a group or individual in your school or community who might feel like outsiders. How can we create a more inclusive environment?

She was surprised to see that everyone in her junior and senior classes had not only turned in their essay on time, but most were at least five pages long, which was impressive for this year's senior class, who tended to slack in their final year. It warmed her heart to read how compassionate and understanding some of their responses were. She found herself smiling as Carrie plopped down opposite her, a takeout bag rustling.

"Ugh, still grading those?" Carrie sighed, pushing aside a stack of papers to make room for the aromatic food. "You're taking your teaching responsibilities *way* too seriously."

"Nice, Care. You're not winning any teacher-of-the-year awards with that attitude."

"I'm just saying, pace yourself, El," Carrie said, dipping back into the bag in search of napkins. "You just got back into the classroom."

"Exactly," Elena said, setting aside the paper she was working on so it wouldn't get greasy. "And I've got a lot to catch up on, as you can see."

"I see that. But you've been burning the midnight oil, and you could use a little break. It's the weekend, for shit's sake," Carrie said. She rustled through the bag and started to pull out food and set it on the desk. "Hey, when's the last time we had movie night?"

Elena raised her eyebrows. "At least three months ago. I think we watched *The Shining*."

"That's right," Carrie said, sliding a box of food in front of Elena. "You kept saying Jack was dead, frozen in the maze—"

"Because he was!" Elena exclaimed.

"—but I said his soul was claimed by the hotel. The final shot with Jack in the 1921 photo says it all. It's pretty obvious."

"Uh, for his soul to have been claimed, he'd have to be dead, right? *That's* pretty obvious."

Carrie thought on it a moment, then said, "Shit, you're right."

They fell silent while they opened the fast food containers and dug into the food. Carrie had gotten takeout from Superdawg's, Elena's favorite. They had the best hotdogs and burgers, garnished with pickled green tomatoes and served in little red boxes with black diamond patterns.

"Let's do it," Elena said, wiping a smear of mustard from the corner of her mouth with a paper napkin.

"What? Movie night?"

"Yeah." Elena hesitated a moment and then said, "But no horror movies. Not the best idea right now."

Concern creased Carrie's brow. "Having the nightmares again?"

Elena shook her head, forcing a smile. "No, nothing like that. It's just...maybe something lighter? A good comedy?"

"Fine, fine," Carrie conceded with a playful pout and took a big bite out of the Whoopercheesie, wiping grease from her chin. "But next movie night, we're absolutely watching *The Thing*. The Kurt Russell version, not the new one with Mary Elizabeth Winstead—though that one's pretty solid. Deal?"

Elena managed a weak laugh. "Deal. How about we invite Maria?"

Carrie's eyes brightened. "Excellent idea! I'll text her right now."

Minutes later, Maria's enthusiastic reply buzzed on Carrie's phone. "She's in! She says 'Pizza and laughs—the perfect antidote to a stressful week.' Oh, and 'Better be deep dish.'"

Later that evening, with the Chicago skyline shimmering through Elena's windows, they set the mood by streaming episodes of *New Girl*, starting back at season one so Carrie could catch up. The aroma of pizza battled with the comforting aroma of scented candles. Elena found herself relaxing for the first time in weeks. As episodes of *New Girl* played in the background, she sipped a glass of red wine and took pleasure out of hearing Carrie laugh at the antics of Jess and the gang.

An hour passed, and Carrie reached for the remote. "I don't know what's taking Maria so long, but I'm going to start the movie."

"No, don't start it yet." Elena swatted playfully at the remote control. "Text her and find out what's taking so long. Tell her the deep dish pizza's getting cold."

Picking up her phone, Carrie's fingers flew across the screen as she typed in her message. "It's Friday night. She's probably hanging out with kids her own age."

"You think she'd rather hang out with catty high school girls than two ancient chicks that used to listen to music on CDs?"

"Wouldn't you?" Carrie said, raising her eyes from the phone.

A sudden buzz from Carrie's phone made them both jump. She glanced at the screen, her brow furrowing. "It's Maria. She says she's...still at the school?"

Elena frowned. "Why would she still be at school on Friday night? Is there a football game or something going on?"

Carrie shrugged and tapped out a reply. Moments later, her eyes widened. "Uh, Elena...you have to see this."

Elena leaned over, a cold dread pooling in her stomach. Carrie held the phone out, the text message stark and chilling: "She's back. And this time, we can't stop her."

The television screen flickered, drawing their attention. In the distorted image reflected back, Elena saw not her own face, but a chilling grin stretching across the familiar features of *la vieja malvada*.

A whisper, barely audible, seemed to snake into the room: "Hello, Elena."

The flickering lights plunged them into darkness. A scream, half-laugh, half-terror, escaped Elena's lips. The silence that followed was heavy, broken only by the frantic pounding of their hearts.

About the Author

Steven Pajak, a Chicago-based author, crafts stories that explore the depths of horror and the human psyche. With a pen that dances on the edges of darkness, Steven brings to life tales that challenge, terrify, and linger in the minds of readers. Drawing inspiration from the urban tapestry of Chicago, his work merges the pulse of city life with the eerie quiet of the shadows lurking within the darkest corners of our minds. Steven invites you into a world where fear meets courage, and the journey through his imagination proves as haunting as it is unforgettable.

facebook.com/StevenPajakAuthor
instagram.com/stevenpajak_official
amazon.com/author/stevenpajak

Made in the USA
Monee, IL
15 March 2024

54570120R10152